"The first time we met I thought you were someone else," Jack said in a soft, sexy voice that reverberated inside of Sophie.

"What was really confusing was that to me, at that time, you were my best friend's wife, who I'd always thought pretty but distant. And then suddenly you'd grown warm and desirable. It really shook me. I can't tell you what a relief it was when you turned out to be...well, you."

"You felt something that soon?"

"We were meant to meet each other. There's a bigger plan for us. Does that sound wacky?"

"Yeah, it does," she said. "But I kind of get it."

"And I can't take my eyes off you," he said, smiling. He leaned forward and kissed her lips, then gently grasped her chin and looked into her eyes. "When the time is right, I want you. All of you. Tell me when the moment arrives that you feel the same way about me and I don't care where we are or what we're doing, I'm going to take your body to places it's never been."

IDENTICAL STRANGER

ALICE SHARPE

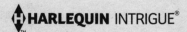

This book is dedicated to Joey, Sam, Koa, Kiwi, Mele, Annie and Bonnie, even though most are no longer with us and none of them could read a word. They each filled our lives and hearts with joy. I mean, really, who doesn't love a dog?

ISBN-13: 978-1-335-60444-6

Identical Stranger

Copyright © 2019 by Alice Sharpe

Recycling programs for this product may not exist in your area.

Printed in U.S.A.

Alice Sharpe met her husband-to-be on a cold, foggy beach in Northern California. Their union has survived the rearing of two children, a handful of earthquakes, numerous cats and a few special dogs, the latest of which is a yellow Lab named Annie Rose. Alice and her husband now live in a small rural town in Oregon, where she devotes the majority of her time to pursuing her second love: writing. You can write to her c/o Harlequin Books, 195 Broadway, 24th Floor, New York, NY 10007. An SASE for reply is appreciated.

Books by Alice Sharpe

Harlequin Intrigue

Hidden Identity
Identical Strangers

The Brothers of Hastings Ridge Ranch

Cowboy Incognito
Cowboy Undercover
Cowboy Secrets
Cowboy Cavalry

The Rescuers

Shattered
Stranded

The Legacy

Undercover Memories
Montana Refuge
Soldier's Redemption

Open Sky Ranch

Westin's Wyoming
Westin's Legacy
Westin Family Ties

Visit the Author Profile page at Harlequin.com.

CAST OF CHARACTERS

Sophie Sparrow—She never dreamed her desire for self-improvement would lead to murder attempts, startling revelations about her past and meeting the love of her life.

Jackson Travers—As an ex-policeman turned private detective, he's repeatedly been touched by violence. This time is different. This time it's Sophie in peril—and he can't fail her.

Sabrina Cromwell—She's disappeared. Did she leave of her own volition or did someone abduct her?

Danny Privet—An attorney with his sights set on Sophie. How far will he go to get her?

Adam Cook—Jack knows he's hiding something. Is it Sabrina?

Louis Nash—A surly photographer with a "no trespassing" attitude. Can they afford to ignore him?

Buzz Cromwell—Everyone knows the husband is always first on the list of suspects when the wife disappears.

Paul Rey—Does this ex-con suffer delusions of grandeur or deeper, darker desires?

Chapter One

Sophie Sparrow sat very still, the sound of rain hitting the window the only noise in the room. As a young girl, she'd imagined what this moment would feel like. Boy, had she been wrong.

"What do you say?" Danny Privet asked as he knelt on bended knee by her side. A glittering diamond ring sparkled in his hand.

She gulped. When he'd asked to come by this Saturday morning, she'd assumed they would go out to brunch. She had not even imagined this. "Danny, I—"

"Go on, say yes," Sophie's mother prompted from her self-imposed semipermanent residence in a recliner located four feet to Sophie's left.

Danny's head swiveled to her mother and then back to Sophie. "If you're worried about having to move to Seattle, don't. I've secured a position here in Portland. My new job starts in two weeks."

"You quit your job! But what's the rush?" Sophie whispered as she tried to make an intimate moment out of a public one. Her long straight hair fell forward if she leaned her head just so, creating an impromptu curtain between her mother and herself where she could study Danny in privacy. Why had he chosen to propose now? What was going on?

For a second, his soft gray eyes held an unfamiliar edge. She'd always wondered how anyone as agreeable as he was could make it as an attorney, how he could defend a client in a court of law, but this new glimpse into his character suggested he possessed the passion a courtroom would require. "Why should we wait?" he responded. "I've known you were the right woman for me since the minute I saw you in that grocery store. Why not get married now?"

"Now?"

"Well, I know how important a wedding is to you ladies. Plan whatever you want, I'll pay for it, just make sure we tie the knot by Wednesday because Thursday morning, we leave for Hawaii! I remember you mentioned wanting to go there. I've already bought the tickets and made all the arrangements. It'll be a honeymoon you'll never forget!"

Sophie would have gulped again if her throat wasn't so dry. She felt like a contestant on a game show, different curtains lifting to reveal unexpected—and in this case, unwanted—surprises. "Oh, Danny, you shouldn't have—"

"For once in your life," her mother interrupted, "use your head. This boy wants to marry you."

"I certainly do," Danny said. "And, frankly, Sophie, I thought you'd jump at the chance."

Sophie, just about speechless, finally mumbled,

"We've only known each other a few weeks. I need more time."

"To wait for a better offer?" her mother scoffed. "Show some spunk! This boy is a wonderful catch, especially for someone of your—well, think about how kind he's been to me. What else do you need?"

I need to love him, Sophie whispered internally, *and I don't. I've been waiting twenty-six years to find someone to complete me, a second half that I've always known existed out there somewhere. Silly? Romantic? Probably, but there you go.*

As usual, when faced with her mother's iron will, Sophie voiced these arguments solely to herself, where they went to work burning a hole in her gut.

"Thank you for your compliments, Margaret," Danny said softly, "but I can't agree with your assessment of Sophie. To me she's a star, the brightest in the heavens, an angel surrounded by a halo of gossamer fawn silk."

Gossamer fawn silk… Did he mean her hair? The flattery sounded like lines lifted from a greeting card, but on the other hand, it was kind of nice to hear positive—if overly flowery—things about herself instead of negative. She smiled appreciation.

Danny apparently mistook her smile for acquiescence. Taking her hand, he slipped the ring on her finger. He got up off his knees and sat down on the sofa beside her, placing himself between Sophie and her mother. He squeezed her hand. The ring was too big and had slipped to the side; the pressure of his grip pinched the stone between her fingers.

"I knew you'd say yes," he said with a smile bordering on a smirk. "I was so confident you'd see how perfect this is that I already bought you a wedding present. You know that house a block over that's for sale? I bought it yesterday. You'll be close enough to keep an eye on your mom."

He'd purchased a ring, a honeymoon and a house before even popping the question and without asking for any input from her. She'd known him about a month. How had he been so sure she'd say yes?

"I've also taken the liberty of looking into hiring full-time live-in help," he added, addressing Margaret. "I hope you don't think it presumptuous of me but I see how you struggle. Would you mind having someone else living here with you?"

Sophie's mother fanned her face with her hand. "I'm just a disabled old widow, Danny. I know you have your own mother to consider. You shouldn't worry about me. But yes, it would be so nice to have someone to talk to who doesn't prattle on about teaching babies how to read. I'll tell you, a little of that goes a long way."

"I think her enthusiasm is cute." Danny chuckled as he squeezed Sophie's hand again.

His condescending words struck her like poison darts. She pulled her hand free as retorts ransacked her stomach looking for real estate in which to sink new geysers.

And how could her mother not understand that the money Sophie made teaching her adorable first-graders was all that stood between this admittedly small house and a tent on the sidewalk?

"What would you like to talk about instead, Mom? Your sciatica? What a big disappointment I am?"

Was that her voice she just heard? Had her thoughts actually forced their way up her throat and out of her mouth? Her gaze darted from Danny's face to her mother's. Their stunned expressions made it crystal clear she had indeed given voice. Dumbfounded, she stared down at the gaudy ring on her finger.

Margaret didn't miss a beat. "Danny, dear, if you haven't changed your mind about marrying bridezilla over there, perhaps you and I should discuss the details."

He leaned forward. "Don't take her words personally, Margaret. She's just excited. A wedding is the most important day of a woman's life, right?"

Their voices faded to white noise. Sophie couldn't feel her feet. In fact, numbness seemed to be spreading up her legs toward her heart.

She stood abruptly, catching both of their attention. Looking from one pair of startled eyes to the next, she mumbled, "I have to go."

"Where?" her mother demanded.

"The school," she said. Where else would she go?

"Since when is the school open on a Saturday? What's gotten into you?"

"It's a…PTA bake sale," she muttered.

"I'll drive you," Danny said, starting to stand.

"No, thanks," she called over her shoulder as she forced her legs to carry her into the kitchen, where she grabbed her coat and purse from the hook by the door and moved quickly outside. Oscar the cat scooted past her into the warmth of the house before she closed the door and ran through the pouring rain to the curb where she'd parked. For once the aging compact started without trouble and she drove down the street with no plan except escape.

After a couple of miles and ever-increasing traffic, she pulled to the curb, turned off the car but kept an iron-fisted grip on the wheel to still her shaking hands.

Her cell rang and Danny's name flashed onto the screen. Damn if she wasn't tempted to answer the call. As soon as it stopped ringing, she picked up the phone and turned off the power.

The panic that had fueled her this far now began escaping into the atmosphere like steam rising from hot bread. She attempted to review the pieces of what had just happened, who said what, all of that, but the words were muted now, details washed out, a blur. What remained was the one moment when she'd glimpsed her life through a different lens and hated what she saw.

Had she run from her mother's negativity, Danny's condescension or her own sudden fear?

A woman exiting a shop caught her attention. Tall and svelte, what really made Sophie look twice was her crown of platinum curls that seemed to announce to the world that this woman took no prisoners. The shop she had left was a hair salon.

"I want to trade places with her," Sophie said aloud. She got out of the car and walked into the salon.

The hairdresser turned as Sophie entered.

"I need help," Sophie said.

"Honey, all I can do is fix your hair," the woman said with a half smile.

"That's a start," Sophie said. And in her heart she knew she could never go back to the way things had been.

JACKSON TRAVERS SAT across the table from the very pretty wife of his best friend, though right now she looked exhausted. It had taken him hours to drive here from his house in Northern California, and as of yet, he still had no idea why Sabrina had summoned him. What he did know was that there wasn't much he wouldn't do for Buzz and, by extension, Buzz's wife.

"It was really nice of you to come," she said after the waitress delivered coffee. "I'm sorry the hotel is so crazy. As far as I know, this is the first February they've hosted a conference here. I had a reservation but I'm worried you're going to have trouble—"

"Don't worry about it. The front desk connected me with a little place a couple of miles down the road, so it's okay. I have to admit I'm curious why you called," he added. "You sounded spooked on the phone."

As she pushed aside her dark hair, a series of fresh red scratches on her forehead caught his attention. Since he'd already noticed the abrasions on her palms when they shook hands and the stiff way she moved as she preceded him into the coffee shop next to the hotel, his curiosity ran rampant. "I've never called a private investigator before," she said.

He flashed what he hoped was an encouraging smile. "Think of it more as calling a friend. I know we've only met a few times, but you're Buzz's wife and that makes you family."

She smiled. "Thanks."

"So..."

"First of all, I don't want Buzz alarmed," she said quickly. "He has enough going on right now."

"You're referring to him being in Antarctica."

"Yes. The whole scientific team is currently aboard a Russian ship visiting outer islands. I can reach him by radio but holding an in-depth conversation is really hard. He doesn't need to worry about me."

Jack studied her for a second. He'd had a feeling of destiny when she called, something not common to him, something he didn't even believe in. He'd just had the sensation that her call was the catalyst of a crucial moment in his life and he'd rearranged his plans to travel here without a second's hesitation. "I can't promise you I won't notify Buzz until I know what we're talking about," he told her at last. "Why don't you just tell me what's going on."

She swallowed a sigh and fidgeted a bit before finally speaking. "It started a couple months ago when I was in the kitchen cooking lasagna. The neighbors across the backyard were having their porch painted. I was at the window draining pasta when I saw the painter taking photos of me with a big camera. By the time I set aside the strainer, his back was to me and then he left... I just had the strangest feeling he'd been doing more than taking pictures, the feeling of, well, invasion."

"You were cooking?"

"Yes."

A painful lump appeared in his throat as her words awakened painful memories. They had no place in the present and he did his best to ignore them. "Why do you use the word *invasion*?"

She shrugged one shoulder. "It felt...personal. Stupid, huh?"

"I don't know," he told her, the lump refusing to budge. "Did he paint the porch?"

"What do you mean?"

"Did he finish the job?"

She thought for a second. "I don't know."

For a second he just stared at her, forcing himself to let go of out-of-context parallels between Sabrina's issues and his own past. She was sitting here, alive, proof that his imagination was getting the worst of him. "What happened next?" he finally said.

"A day or so later I came home from work to the feeling that someone had just left our house. No one was there, of course, but I swear, there was just some lingering essence, something that sent chills up my spine. It happened the next day, too. I searched the house but nothing was missing, nothing was even out of place. There was just...nothing."

"Did you call the cops?"

"Of course not. What could they do?"

"Well, something made you uneasy," Jack said, not only to reassure her but because he was a firm believer that reasonable people picked up on offbeat vibes they sometimes couldn't even identify.

"I run into burning buildings for a living," she said

softly. "I'm not anxious to be tagged as the woman who gets rattled over nothing."

"Buzz calls you unflappable," he said.

She smiled fondly.

"Anything else?"

"Just that same watched feeling. It started to get under my skin. Last weekend when I walked out of the fire station it was stronger than ever. I looked around, but the only person I saw was sitting in a parked car. He immediately drove off but that afternoon I came home from work and found an origami fox folded out of a dollar bill sitting on the front porch."

Again he stared at her because now the vibe had changed from creepy to sophomoric. *No*, he cautioned himself, *her story is just diverging from the one written in your head. This is her story, not a trashy remake of yours.* "Not inside the house?" he said aloud. "No note or anything?"

"Nothing."

He folded his hands around his cup. "Tell me why we're meeting here in Seaport and not back in Astoria where all of this happened."

"I'm not sure you know this or not, but every February for years I've driven up and down the coast. There aren't many tourists in the winter and the hiking trails are all but empty. Anyway, after Buzz and I got married, we took the trip together. I was dragging my feet about it this year because Buzz is gone, but after I found one of those origami foxes perched on my steering wheel I decided it was time to get away for a while, and since I'd already made all the reservations—well, I just went, a day early, too, which I thought would give me a chance to chill out.

"I drove down to the California border pretty much in a straight line, stayed a couple of nights in Brookings and then started my way back up the coast just like I always do. Everything was going okay until I was hiking a narrow trail down to the beach about fifty miles south of here. A falling boulder appeared out of nowhere. It hit my left side and knocked me to the ground. I had to scramble to keep from going over the edge. It was a long way down to the rocks and I could hear waves breaking." She took a deep breath and continued. "Once I was back on the trail I heard something on the bluff above me."

"Like what?" he asked as he realized the scratches on her face and hands were undoubtedly caused when she fought to keep from tumbling over the edge of the mountain.

"Like footsteps."

"You're thinking some purposely dislodged the rock?"

"I don't know…maybe."

"Did you report the incident to authorities?"

She shook her head. "I climbed up to take a look myself. The spot was within easy walking distance of the parking lot. No one was around. The ground was muddy after this run of wet weather but it was also covered with pebbles—I couldn't see any footprints. What could the police do?"

"Investigate," he said gently. "Also, they'd be in the position to tell you if similar incidents had happened to other hikers due to weather or even vandals. They might have been able to help you understand if the falling rock was personal or accidental."

"Okay, you make a point. But I keep thinking police will question friends and acquaintances and word will get back to Buzz. What's he supposed to do from half a world away and what if the paper foxes are just some stupid prank? Anyway, I woke up ridiculously early this morning and ordered room service to be left in the hall while I took a shower." She retrieved her purse from the floor beside her, grabbed something from its depths and showed it to Jack. "This was on the tray when I uncovered it."

Resting on her deeply scratched palm he found an origami fox folded out of a dollar bill. "I called Housekeeping at once to see if they'd put it there," she continued. "They hadn't, of course. I put the tray back in the hall and called you. Then I left. Once it was light, I stopped for a long walk on the beach. Nothing happened and I almost called you back to cancel but I figured you were already on your way.

"So anyway, I drove to Seaport. I always stay at this hotel and I thought if you and I met here, you could help me figure things out. After I checked in I went up to my room to collapse but the maid wasn't finished cleaning so I came back to the dining room for breakfast. While I was waiting for my order, a man walked into the restaurant, made eye contact with me and immediately took a seat at the bar. I swear he was staying at the same hotel I was at when the rock fell. His being here could be sheer coincidence, of course, except that I have a feeling I've also seen him in Astoria."

"Did you talk to him?"

She shook her head.

"Could he be the painter from your neighbor's porch?"

She thought for a moment. "No. This guy had light brown hair and a trimmed beard… The painter was taller, darker, bigger. And maybe older."

"How about the guy you glimpsed in the parked car?"

She thought again. "Really hard to tell. By the time my backbone rebuilt itself this morning, the man had left the restaurant." She rubbed her eyes and took a deep breath. "If this guy is following me and leaving little gifts, I want to know it before I get home and he invades my house again or drops another rock on my head." She took another breath before adding, "Jack, I know it's a lot to ask but do you think you could help me confront him?"

"Of course. And if it turns out he's just a hapless traveler, I'll drive back to Astoria with you and see what we can do there. First we have to find this guy."

"And you won't tell Buzz."

"We'll leave him out of it as long as we can. That's all I can promise." He didn't add the same deal would exist concerning police involvement.

"Okay."

"And I have to ask. Could anyone you know be behind all this?"

"What? No!"

"Someone you don't know well, then, someone with whom you're in a legal battle."

"Legal battle?"

"Well, the origami is folded out of money, right? Why? Could it be because someone thinks you or Buzz owe them something?"

She shook her head. "Neither one of us is in any kind of argument with anyone, legal or not. Buzz's friends are all scientists more concerned with sea ice extent than money and none of them live locally. My friends are firefighters. They're family to me. I'm an only child. My parents are deceased. I'm alone in the world, really, except for Buzz."

"And Buzz wasn't having trouble with anyone before he left?"

"No. None of this makes any sense and that makes me think it's all in my head."

"The origami fox isn't in your head," he reminded her.

She rubbed her eyes. "No, it's not."

"Nor was the falling rock."

She looked unsure about that but he wasn't a big fan of coincidences. The boulder could easily have killed her—probably would have if she wasn't in tip-top shape.

And that meant someone wanted her dead.

"I have an idea," he told her. "Why don't I take photos of the men in this hotel while you get some rest. You can look at the pictures later and we'll go from there."

She started to argue with him, but he stood firm. Her eyes were bloodshot and she kept rolling her shoulders as though yesterday's fall had hurt her neck or back. "Please, Sabrina. Get some sleep. In the long run, it will make everything go faster. Trust me."

She finally agreed and he insisted on escorting her to her hotel next door and upstairs. They exited the elevator and turned toward the long, beige hall as a man in coveralls carrying a toolbox entered the freight elevator a few steps away. Jack heard the whirring of the motor as it descended.

"Where's your luggage?" he asked after Sabrina had opened her door and he'd preceded her into her room.

"Still in my car."

He checked the locked door to the balcony, the bathroom and the closet. "What are you driving?"

"Buzz's old SUV. Why?"

"If you'll give me your keys I'll run down and get your things for you," he told her.

"All I want to do is climb under those blankets and sleep. I'll get everything later."

"Okay, but don't forget to slide the dead bolt after me," he added and fervently hoped that when this was all said and done, Buzz would understand why Jack didn't immediately get ahold of him no matter where he was.

Before he settled into a good chair in the lobby, he bought a cup of coffee at a kiosk he suspected had been created to service the dozens of human resource conference attendees milling around the hotel. As far as dropping everything to drive here, that hadn't been all that hard. He was in the middle of two cases but he got a buddy to cover one and the other could simmer a couple of days. The only other thing he'd had to do was cancel a date he hadn't been real interested in going on anyway.

Phone on camera mode, he clandestinely began taking pictures of every adult male he saw, customer or employee, bearded or clean shaven, tagged with a conference badge or not. Some of them seemed highly unlikely when compared with the brief description Sabrina had given—no facial hair, too heavy or tall or short—but all those things could be altered by a clever con man.

He'd just returned from his second run to the coffee kiosk when his roving gaze took in Sabrina moving away from the check-in desk. He set the coffee aside and walked over in time to catch her halfway to the door. "There you are. Ready to look at the pictures I took while you snoozed away the afternoon?" She had changed clothes, put on a coat and acquired a smattering of raindrops in her hair and on her shoulders. She'd been outside? She must have gone out to her car to retrieve her luggage. How had he missed her leaving the hotel, coming back inside to change and then apparently leaving again?

"I beg your pardon?" she said.

He finally looked past the raindrops. "I stand corrected," he said. "You skipped the nap and went to a salon instead. I hear that can be just as fortifying."

Her hand flew up to touch the lilac strands running through her glossy dark hair. "What I did with my afternoon is none of your business," she said with a defiant tilt of her chin and then ruined the effect by shrinking back. "I'm sorry. That was rude." She raised her hand as if to pat her hair and dropped it. "Does it look as bad as I think?"

He rushed to assure her. "It looks just like it did before, right, except for the purple streak?"

His words were met by another alarmed expression. "It's two shades darker and ten inches shorter." Her brow furled. "I'm sorry," she said again. "I've been in such a fog today. I'm having the hardest time placing how we know each other. Who are you?"

"Who am I? Are you sleepwalking?" She didn't smile at his attempt at humor. "Okay," he said in a more serious tone. "How about letting me in on the joke."

"Danny has something to do with this, doesn't he?" she said as she glanced around the lobby. "He's not here, is he? Please, tell me he's not here."

"How could he be here?" He shook his head to clear it. Was it even remotely possible that Buzz's wife had a split personality? Had recent stress caused some kind of abnormal blip in her psyche? He touched her shoulder. "Are you sure you're okay? Did you change your mind and call Buzz, I mean Danny, after all?"

She held up one hand. "Wait a second. Why would I call him when all I want is a little space to think? And for that matter, why did you call Danny Buzz?"

"He earned the nickname two decades ago when he knocked a beehive out of a tree and got stung thirteen times, which is why he always carries epinephrine with him—just a second, he never told you about the bees?"

"No. This happened when he was growing up outside Seattle?"

He felt like scratching his head. "Buzz grew up across the street from my house in Napa, California."

"He told me he grew up in Seattle," she said.

"Why would he do that?"

"How should I know? He said his stepfather piloted a ferry on Puget Sound and his mom was—is—a housekeeper. He and his younger half brother—wait a second, why did Danny send you here instead of coming himself?"

Something weird was going on. He lowered his voice as they'd begun to draw attention. "You called me, remember? You asked me to meet you here. You've been feeling threatened and you asked for help figuring things out. You went up to take a nap—"

"I can't even get a room here."

He studied her face for some sign she was messing with him, dissecting her delicate features, aware as he did so that she flinched under the scrutiny, obviously uncomfortable and ready to run. She tried to rake her hair over her face but it was too short.

What was happening? This was the same woman he'd watched walk down the aisle two years earlier to marry his best friend, the same woman who sat across from him two hours before desperate for his help. And yet, somehow, it wasn't her either. She "felt" different, like a lost and impotent version of herself. Two hours ago she'd been Buzz's wife and now she was a complete stranger.

"Did Danny cook this up?" she said in a whisper, and he could feel her anxiety leap to a new level. "Mother must have guessed I'd come here—but why send a stranger?" She looked toward the door before turning back to meet his gaze. "I'd really appreciate it if you'd stop pretending you know me and just be honest."

"Wait a second," he said, ignoring the fact that she'd mentioned her mother in the present tense when the woman had died years before, ignoring everything except her unmarred forehead. "Where are the scratches?"

"What scratches?"

"The ones you got when that boulder fell. Let me see your hands." He caught her left hand before she could move away. "Nothing," he murmured as he studied her palm. Her hand trembled in his grip and he released it. "Where's your wedding band?"

"Do you mean that stupid engagement ring? Because that's in my purse."

"I'm talking about the wedding band Buzz gave you. It belonged to his grandmother." He shook his head. "Sabrina, something is very wrong."

"My name's not Sabrina."

He peered into her deep brown eyes and finally accepted she was as clueless as he was. With the realization came a giant wave of relief. Sabrina hadn't morphed into a delusional head case and he hadn't fantasized that her very essence had changed.

The relief was short-lived as the woman standing inches away narrowed her eyes. But when she spoke, her voice was soft. "Don't you think it's time you explained what's going on?"

"I wish I could," he said.

Chapter Two

Oblivious to the hustle and bustle of the lobby around her, Sophie perched on the edge of an off-white chair and studied the man who had accosted her.

There was no denying he was better-looking than about 98 percent of the men currently walking on planet Earth, but if there was one thing she'd learned the hard way it was this: looks mattered exactly zero. What good were broad shoulders, a lean, fit body and very blue eyes if the person sporting these attributes turned out to be a lunatic or a manipulator...or both?

"I can't believe you're not Sabrina," he said. "The likeness is incredible."

"First things first," she said. "Just who are you?"

"My name is Jack Travers. I'm a private investigator from California."

"For real?"

"Yeah," he said. "Why does that surprise you?"

"I don't know. I guess you don't look like one."

"What does one look like?" he asked.

"Humphrey Bogart," she answered without hesitation.

"Isn't he a little dated for you?"

"My mother watches a ton of cable TV. I grew up watching *The Maltese Falcon*."

"That's a hard act to follow. Now, who are you?"

"Sophia Sparrow. Sophie. When you say this woman and I look alike, you're talking in general terms?"

"Like eye color and height?" he asked and shook his head. "No. I mean identical, like clones, like twins. In fact, that's the only explanation for your startling similarities and why I was so sure you were her."

"Except that I don't even have a sister let alone a twin," she said. "In fact, I'm an only child."

"So is Sabrina."

"You said she's your friend's wife?"

"Yes."

"You also said she felt threatened. What's wrong? Is she in trouble?"

"I think so, yes," he said, "but she talked to me in confidence so I won't go into details."

"You also mentioned a falling boulder."

"Did I?"

Sophie wished he would stop staring at her. She tilted her head but no hair fell forward. Why had she chosen today of all days to cut it? She studied her hands to escape his gaze but looked back up because she wanted to know what he was thinking and so far she wasn't sure. She only knew it was important to figure it out. Something strange was going on in many ways at the same time, leaving her confused and worried.

She'd driven to the coast for one reason—to think. And yet in the back of her mind she admitted that thinking about this mix-up was easier than thinking about herself.

With what sounded like an aha, Jack took his phone out of his pocket and fooled around with it for a second, then turned it so she could see the screen. "This is a photo I took at Sabrina's wedding. The groom is my friend Daniel Cromwell. He's currently in Antarctica. Take a look at the bride's face."

Sophie glanced from Jack's intense gaze to the picture, and in that instant, her world flipped on its axis—again. From the bride's small cowlick near her hairline to her heavily lashed dark eyes, from the shape of her face to her eyebrows to the bump on her nose, everything Sophie could see looked familiar.

Was this a trick? Had an old picture of Sophie somehow been Photoshopped into this format? So many things were different—hairstyle, hair color, makeup, jewelry, dress and, oh yeah, what little she could see of a dark-haired guy whose face was smashed up against hers. This was not a photo of Sophie and yet it looked as though it was.

"She's prettier than me," Sophie said.

"She's a duplicate of you," Jack murmured, his glance darting from the telephone to Sophie. "And you're a duplicate of her."

"She doesn't have a mole on her cheek like I do," Sophie continued, unable to stop staring at the woman on the screen. "Does she color her hair?"

"I don't know. Except that she doesn't have a purple streak."

"Neither did I until this morning. You said her name is Sabrina?"

"Yeah. Sabrina Cromwell. Her maiden name was Long. Sabrina Long. She grew up in Astoria, Oregon, about sixty minutes north of here. How about you?"

Sophie had been digging in her shoulder bag as he spoke and now produced her wallet. She handed him her driver's license. "Born and raised in Portland, Oregon. How old is Sabrina?"

"Eight years younger than Buzz, so around twenty-six or so. Wait, I remember Buzz saying she's a July baby." He scanned her driver's license. "Looks like you were born in July, too."

"Lots of people are born in July," she said as she continued staring at Sabrina's face.

He dug in his pocket and produced his own wallet. "You don't have to take me on face value either," he said, handing her his driver's and private investigator's licenses. She looked them over before returning them. "Are you adopted?" he asked.

"No. Is she?"

"Not that I know of."

"I want to meet her."

"I think she'll want to meet you, too, but I'm pretty sure she turned her phone off when she decided to take a nap. I'll try calling her room."

Sophie popped to her feet. "She's here, in this hotel, right now?"

"Yes."

She blinked several times. Was she up to more shocks and surprises? Did she have a choice? She followed Jack to the desk, where he placed the call but ended up leaving a message. "I'm going upstairs to check on her," Jack said. "I'll be right back."

"May I come with you?" Sophie squeaked, then stiffened her resolve. "I need to see her with my own eyes. This is all so...weird."

"I think she'll need a few minutes to adjust to... things. She's pretty stressed."

"Yeah, well, so am I."

He smiled and the transformation was stunning. Half-surreal before, he now turned into a genuine human being. "I can see how you'd feel that way," he said, and together they rode up to the third floor and walked down the hall.

He finally stopped and knocked on the door of room 302. It was the same room Sophie had stayed in the summer before, the one she'd hoped to get today because it had a great view of the beach. They waited a few seconds and then he knocked again, harder this time. He twisted the knob to no effect. "I'm going to try a credit card," he said as he opened his wallet.

"Shouldn't we just go downstairs and ask for help?"

"Probably, but it's chancy they'll open the door without provocation. I saw this in a movie. It might work, what the heck."

As he ran a variety of cards through the magnetic lock, Sophie heard footsteps and glanced up to find a maid carrying an armload of towels walking toward them. She elbowed Jack, who glanced over his shoulder and quickly stuck the cards in his pockets. Sophie looked back at the maid in time to see a man turn the corner on his way to the elevator. He and Sophie made eye contact. He stopped dead in his tracks. His gaze shifted as he patted his pockets, then he turned on his heels and disappeared back around the corner.

It looked as though he'd forgotten something.

The housekeeper paused midstep. "I saw you earlier today," she said, smiling at Sophie. "Did you leave your key in your room?"

"Yes," Sophie said. The woman had mistaken her for Sabrina Cromwell. The last possibility that Jack might be in cahoots with Danny in some elaborate scheme to accomplish heaven knew what toppled off the edge of probability.

"I can open it for you," the woman said. For a second, Sophie wondered how they would explain the sleeping woman already in the room, but the bed was empty and the maid went on her way.

They closed the door behind them.

Jack glanced at the open door of the bathroom as he strode to the balcony and tried the glass door. It was locked. Planting his hands on his waist, he stated the obvious. "She's not here."

"Where are her things?" Sophie asked because aside from a rumpled bed and a damp hand towel in the bathroom, the room looked untouched.

"In her car. I guess I should go make sure it's still parked outside. Give me your cell number and I'll call you when I get this cleared up."

The impulse to wait in the lobby drew her like a magnet. She could find a corner where she could commence thinking about her life. Waiting felt comfortable. It felt natural.

She looked up into Jack's blue eyes. The anxiety

she found there made waiting seem an inconceivable option. "You think something happened to her," she stated flatly.

"I don't see how it could have, but yeah, I'm concerned."

"Then I'm coming with you."

"You don't need to do that. I'll let you know."

"Listen," Sophie said, reaching over to grasp his arm, then removing her hand at once. There must be something on his jacket sleeve, some invisible substance that made her palms tingle. "There aren't any rooms available at the hotel, I'm not going home and I'm not going to risk losing track of you and Sabrina. It's like fate is screaming my name, trying to tell me something. Normally I would ignore such unwanted callouts from things like destiny and all that, but today— I don't know, I think I should listen. I can't explain it, I just have to find out where Sabrina is, who she is. I have to *see* her." She shrugged and slid him a glance to see if he was ready to bolt. He actually nodded and she took a deep breath. "I don't understand how anyone can look so much like me and not actually be—" She stopped short.

"Related," he finished for her and briefly touched her arm as though he understood. "Nor do I. All right, come with me. Let's see if we can find her car."

"She's driving Buzz's old Chevy," he said as they walked out into the rainy afternoon. "Think rusty hulk."

He pulled the hood up on his jacket. She hesitated

while still under the protection of the portico, and he realized her coat didn't have a hood and the rain had done nothing but go from bad to worse. "Why don't you wait here while I check the outside lot, then if need be, we can look in the parking garage together."

"Okay," she agreed.

Ten minutes later he jogged back to the front of the hotel to find Sophie gone. Man, he was losing women left and right today, but in this case, he thought it likely Sophie Sparrow had rethought her involvement with this situation and cut her loses. He was disappointed and not only because he was curious about the connection between her and Sabrina. Maybe it was for the better. What good could possibly come from being attracted to a woman who lived hours away, looked just like his best friend's wife and, more to the point, was in the middle of a relationship with a guy named Danny?

Was he attracted? Yeah, for whatever reason, he was. He wanted to know why she'd stuck purple in her hair. He wanted to know why she was timid one minute and brave the next.

Bypassing the valet's offer of help, he entered the parking garage located under the hotel.

Sophie was waiting for him inside the entrance. He was able to stifle the smile that threatened to curve his lips, but there wasn't a thing he could do about the spark of pleasure that flared in his chest.

"It was cold standing out there," she said as she joined him. "It's not much warmer in here, though. I take it her car isn't in the lot?"

"No. Let's work our way down."

But search as they might, they could not find a rusty white Chevy SUV with a red stripe down its side in among all the sleeker, newer models. By the time they reached the bottom tier, Jack was sure Buzz's car wasn't parked in either the lot or the garage. That meant Sabrina had driven it away from the hotel. Why? What caused her to leave without telling him? It seemed so out of character.

He took out his cell to try Sabrina again but the reception was nonexistent down here.

"Let's go back up to the lobby and see if I can get some coverage. Obviously Sabrina left the hotel for some reason. I guess she couldn't find me to explain why. I'll call her again."

Sophie had to know as well as he that his words didn't explain why she didn't call or text or why she wasn't responding to his repeated attempts to contact her. She nodded but made no comment.

He started up the ramp, unaware until he was nearing the ground floor that Sophie wasn't directly behind him. He turned to look for her right as revving engine noises bellowed up from below. A human scream came right before four thousand pounds of screeching metal shot past Jack and accelerated up the last ramp, leaving behind the acrid smell of burned rubber.

Jack ran back down the ramp half-sick at what he might find. "Sophie?"

She was plastered to one of the brick support pillars, eyes closed, shaking like a leaf. She was missing her right shoe, and her handbag had disappeared from her shoulder. He clutched her arms. Her eyes flew open, and for a second she stared at him as if she'd never seen him before. Then she burst into tears and fell against his chest.

A few seconds later, pounding footsteps heralded the arrival of the parking valet, who stopped short in his tracks and stared at them as he gasped for breath.

"Is everyone here okay?" he finally managed to sputter.

Jack titled Sophie's chin up. Her brown eyes were huge but a resolute expression had begun to chase away the initial fright. "How about it? Are you all right? Are you hurt?"

She shook her head. "No."

"Are you sure?"

"Shaken but recovering," she muttered.

"What happened?"

With a glance at the valet, who seemed to be hanging on their every word, she shook her head again. "Later."

The valet was not as reticent. "I heard a racket down here and then a car came flying out going ninety miles an hour!" he said, his eyes as round as hubcaps. "I thought for sure someone had been run over flatter than a pancake."

"Did you get a license plate number?" Jack asked.

"Are you kidding?"

"How about a glimpse of the driver?"

"As I was ducking out of the way for my life? Nope."

"Was it a car you'd parked?"

"Doubt it. We have valet spaces reserved on the first floor so we can deliver as fast as possible. If it came from down here, chances are good someone parked it themselves."

"How long have you been on duty?" Jack asked.

"Since morning. I'm going home soon."

"Then do you remember a woman who looked a lot like Ms. Sparrow here parking an older white SUV Chevy?"

"Or taking it out," Sophie added, her voice shaky.

"No. I haven't seen a car like that, not that I remember anyway. There's a parking lot outside. Some people prefer to use that no matter what the weather. Some people really don't like underground garages."

"I may now be one of them," Sophie mumbled, then took a deep breath and straightened up, pushing herself away from Jack's grasp. "I've lost my shoulder bag and my phone," she announced, nose and eyes dripping.

"I'll find them," the valet said, and went to work searching for the bag. With a triumphant whoop, the kid found her purse on top of a car parked a few spaces away and retrieved it. He handed it to Jack, who pressed it into Sophie's hands.

Sophie opened the purse and withdrew a tissue to wipe at her face.

"I'll look for your shoe," the valet offered as he scanned the pavement and kept talking. "You know, we get some awful drivers here, we really do, but this guy took the cake." He leaned way over to shine a penlight under a row of vehicles. He stood again and turned to search the other direction. "That dude peeled out of here like the cops were after him." He knelt again to shine his light. "Found it!" he called as he all but crawled under a van. He stood up grasping the shoe and focused the narrow beam of light on the skid marks scorching the pavement. "I guess you're just lucky he was a good enough driver to miss hitting you," he said as he handed the shoe to Sophie.

Sophie's lips parted. Jack thought she was going to say something but instead she slipped the black loafer on her foot as he steadied her arm.

"Do you have your phone on you?" he asked the valet.

"Sure."

"Sophie, give him your number. Let's see if your phone will ring."

"Good thing I turned it back on," she said as she rattled off her number.

A second later they heard a ring that Jack tracked down to the far side of the garage, where he found it had landed against the tire of a truck. As he picked it up and glanced at the lit screen, he saw numerous alerts that "Danny" had called. He handed it back to Sophie. She scanned the screen momentarily before turning the device off and shoving it in her pocket.

"Let's get out of here," she said as she settled her handbag on her shoulder.

"Sure."

She waited until the valet was far ahead of them before tugging on Jack's sleeve. "The car didn't veer to avoid me," she said. "It swerved to hit me."

"WHY DID YOU wait to tell me that?" Jack asked as they took their first deep breath of fresh ocean air.

The rain Sophie had previously avoided now created a welcome cleansing, and she closed her eyes to turn her face upward.

"Sophie?"

She let Jack lead her under the portico, relieved when the valet left to help an arriving customer. "I don't know," she said. "I guess I didn't want to make a fuss."

He looked down at her as if to speak, but his expression suddenly softened. With one finger he touched her cheek. A raindrop glistened on his fingertip and he met her gaze. It was a strange moment full of currents Sophie didn't understand, but that was okay. This whole day had been a time out of time, one bewildering moment following another.

"Jack?" she finally said.

He blinked away whatever place he'd been lost in. "You sound just like Sabrina," he said. "She didn't want to make a fuss either. And now she's gone."

"Well, I'm right here. Weren't you going to try calling her again?"

He pulled out his phone and a moment later shook his head. "It goes right to voice mail."

They walked back into the lobby. Feeling shaky, Sophie took a chair by the door as Jack continued on to the front desk.

After leaving the hairdresser, she'd headed to Seaport almost on autopilot. This town and this hotel were familiar—she'd been vacationing here for years, first with her parents and then alone after she graduated from college. She'd felt sure this was the place she could figure things out before returning to Portland and explaining herself to Danny and her mother.

In light of what had happened within the last hour, that plan now seemed ancient.

She thought again to the parking garage—could she be mistaken about the driver's intentions?

Jack sat down next to her. "Sabrina is still not answering her room phone, her own phone, anything. I've called the town's other hotels and the hospital. The front desk has no record of her checking out. She's just vanished."

"People don't just vanish," Sophie said.

She saw him flinch and wondered what nerve she'd inadvertently touched. "Actually, people do," he said softly. "At least for a while, sometimes forever." He seemed to shake off whatever had distressed him and leaned toward her. "Tell me why you stayed down on the bottom level of the garage and what happened between the time I left and returned."

"You said something about your phone reception and I stopped to dig my phone out of my purse, turn it on and offer it to you," she began. "Then I became aware that an engine had started and I turned around. A whitish car inched out of its spot, then turned and started my way. I was still standing in the middle of the lane so I moved aside. The driver gunned the engine and the car sped up. I dodged farther right—that's when I think I lost my shoe, but the car veered, too, so I tried to get behind the support. As I ran, I think my bag slipped down my arm and then the car tore it out of my hand. It made the corner with screeching brakes and shot upward toward you. I thought it might hit you… I just stood there like an idiot, too rattled to move. And then there you were—well, you know the rest."

"You felt the attack was purposeful?"

She nodded. "Yes."

"Did you see the driver?"

"Kind of."

"Kind of?"

"I think he was about my age. I don't know—it was a blur."

"Sophie, think carefully, does anyone know you're here?"

"In Seaport? No."

"Think for a little longer. You must have told someone you were coming to the coast."

"*I* didn't even know I was coming until I was practically here."

"Okay, you said something about your mother guessing where you were and you've mentioned a guy named Danny a few times."

"My mother could have guessed. I don't know that she did, but she might have."

"Would she have told Danny?"

"If he asked. But he would never try to run me down."

"You positive?"

She thought for a second. "Yes. He's my boyfriend. Sort of. Probably not anymore. He asked me to marry him this morning and I kind of…left. That's no reason to kill someone."

"You'd be surprised," Jack said.

"Come on," she joked as she resisted the urge to elbow him. "Look at me. I'm not the kind of woman to excite men to grand passion."

"You underestimate yourself," he said. "Okay, we're going to the police."

"Why would we—"

"Because you look exactly like Sabrina. If someone wasn't going after you specifically, then it figures they mistook you for her. The next step could be a great big rock falling on your head. Don't argue with me."

She broke into laughter. "You know, that whacko might have been after you, not me *or* Sabrina."

"He didn't aim at me," Jack said softly.

"Oh. Well, since Sabrina is missing, I think going to the police is a reasonable thing to do."

"So glad you agree," he said with sarcasm and she laughed again. She never laughed like this. Obviously the day's events were catching up with her.

They took Jack's car and within minutes were speaking to an anxious-looking police sergeant who kept glancing at the clock. Jack and Sophie both produced their identification and the sergeant looked it over without much interest until he got to Jack's PI license. "Just out of curiosity, were you formerly military or civil police?" he asked.

"I was a cop in Los Angeles for seven years before going out on my own," Jack said.

"I know a guy who did that, too," the sergeant said as he handed back their papers with a quick peek at the wall clock. "What can I do for you folks?"

Sophie was content to let Jack explain her garage

encounter. He didn't mention that they'd been searching for Sabrina's vehicle but she figured he'd get around to it eventually.

"Ah, this stuff happens all the time," Sergeant Jones said with another glance at the time and a general shuffling of papers. When he saw their interest in his obsession with the clock, he smiled. "It's my tenth anniversary," he confided. "I completely forgot about it last year, and let me tell you, my friends, that is not a mistake I am ever going to make again. I made a reservation at her favorite restaurant but I keep thinking I should do something else. She's always complaining about how old her mixer is—"

"Don't get her an appliance," Sophie interrupted.

"Really?"

Sophie nodded.

"Buy her flowers," Jack said, and Sophie looked at him in surprise. He smiled. "Red roses for passion," he added as he met her gaze.

The sergeant grinned. "Yeah, and I can pick those up at the grocery store on my way home. Now, what was I saying?"

Sophie spoke up. "Jack just told you about the driver who almost—"

"Oh, yeah. I remember. Thing is, some stupid kid gets all excited because he sees a pretty girl and wants to impress her but he's not nearly as cool as he thinks he is and goes too far." He glanced at Jack and added, "And you feel protective, of course, because she's your girl."

Sophie opened her mouth, but Jack jumped in. "I

hope that's all it is," he said. "The guy could have killed her, you know."

Now the policeman glanced at Sophie again. "I wouldn't worry about this, Ms. Sparrow. You aren't hurt, right? And without an ID on the car, there's really not much I can do. I mean, do you have any idea how many newish white sedans are running around in this city?"

Sophie thanked him—for what, exactly? she wondered—and started to stand. That's when Jack brought up Sabrina and revealed what she thought must be the minimal amount to drive home the fact that the woman felt threatened enough to elicit Jack's help. "We were searching for her car when the incident with the wild driver occurred. It's important to remember that Sabrina Cromwell and Sophie Sparrow look very much alike and that Sabrina seems to be missing."

The sergeant once again checked the clock before stifling a sigh. "Did you find her car?"

"No."

Sergeant Jones made a few notes. "Do you have her plate number?"

"It's her husband's SUV so run Daniel Thorne Cromwell, Astoria, Oregon."

"Okay," Jones said as he jotted notes. "We'll keep our eyes open, but honestly, people like this are usually off looking at the beach or shopping or something. You know this, Mr. Travers, from your own experience both as a policeman and as a detective. Chances are good she'll show up. She's an adult, right? No law says she can't get a wild hair. There was no sign of a struggle?"

"No," Jack said.

"Nobody at the hotel is alarmed?"

"No."

"Did you check the hospital?"

"Earlier today."

He made a note. "I'll check again just to be on the safe side. If I learn anything, I'll let you know." The sergeant looked over at the wall clock and they finally took the hint.

Once again they found themselves outside as overhead lights glittered on falling drops of silver rain.

"Why didn't you tell him about Sabrina and the rock?" she asked as he opened the passenger door.

"Because I promised her I'd keep everything she told me quiet as long as I can. I'm doing my best. She's concerned about her husband finding out. He's a long ways away right now."

"In Antarctica," Sophie remembered his saying. "Doing what?"

"He's part of an international team of biologists and other scientists investigating climatic changes. He's been gone a couple of months. Sabrina doesn't want him to worry."

"How do you feel about that?"

"I feel that the stakes have changed. I feel Sabrina needs help and it's clear to me that it's not going to come from Sergeant Jones. He's right that most people who leave suddenly and without explanation usually have a good reason. But most people haven't been followed for days or felt invaded enough to ask for professional help."

"She must have been terrified," Sophie said softly.

He ran a hand through his gorgeous hair and looked her in the eye. "The bottom line is that right now it's clear we represent her best chance of being found."

She noticed he used the word *we*, and as good as it made her feel inside, it frightened her, too. Was she up to the task? Well, she would just have to be. "You're really worried about her," she whispered.

"Yeah," he said, "I am."

Chapter Three

"I forgot about the photos," Jack said as he took his phone out of his jacket pocket. They had just entered the hotel again; maybe that's why he'd finally thought about all the pictures he'd taken earlier today. He and Sophie sat in the lobby once again, only it was now wine and cheese happy hour. While he called up photos, she jumped up to peruse the selection. He also called the hotel Sabrina had mentioned staying at the previous night after her encounter with the rock. What if she'd returned to it for some reason? But the hotel hadn't seen or heard from her since she left earlier that day. Another dead end.

"Things are really picked over," Sophie said as she returned with a tiny cluster of grapes and a couple of crackers. "Tell me about these photos."

"While Sabrina supposedly napped," he explained, "I took pictures of every male I saw. Maybe you'll recognize the driver who almost ran you down. If I photographed him earlier today. He may be a guest here and we may be able to get a name."

She perched on the arm of his overstuffed chair as

he scrolled through the more than four dozen cameos he'd taken. "Wow, you didn't miss a beat," she said when a picture of a ten-year-old kid with his mother showed up.

"I thought it might amuse Sabrina. She was so upset I was hoping to get her to smile."

"How well do you know her?" Sophie asked.

"I met her when Buzz and she first got serious and then again at their engagement party. I was Buzz's best man at their wedding and then I stayed with them one night while I was on my way up to Canada on a case. That was last November, before Buzz left for Antarctica. So, to answer your question, not real well. Today was the longest time she and I have ever talked without someone else around."

He'd been scrolling while they spoke and now she said, "Stop. Go back one. One more. There."

"The guy in the hoodie?"

"Yeah."

He looked up at her, alarmed by how often he had to fight the urge to touch her hand or bump her shoulder. It had been a long time since he'd been flooded with impulses so old-fashioned and innocent yet fueled by such desire. Years in fact, ever since Lisa.

Did Sophie remind him of Lisa? Is that what drew him to her? He didn't know for sure.

Now was not the time to give in to retrograde musings. He put aside random thoughts as he casually said, "This is the man who attempted to run you down?"

"No. This is the guy I saw upstairs outside Sabrina's room right before the maid opened the door for us. He came around the corner behind her. He looked at me for a second and then acted as though he'd forgotten something. He turned around and went back the way he'd come. He wasn't wearing a hoodie then. I think he had light brown hair."

"Sounds pretty innocuous," Jack said.

"Yeah. But there was something kind of strange about the whole thing, too," Sophie said. "The more I think about it, the more I get the feeling he recognized me." She shook her head. "Maybe he'd just seen Sabrina enter her room earlier in the day and thought I was her."

"Sabrina talked about seeing a man in the restaurant this morning," Jack mused. "She was sure she recognized him but she also mentioned he had a beard."

"This guy was clean shaven."

"Beards can be shaved off or fake ones can be applied with adhesive," Jack said.

"That's true. So we're at…nowhere?"

"I'm not sure. The first thing to do is ID this guy."

"How?"

"The valet, the people at the desk. If the guy was upstairs in the hall, then he probably has a room here. We'll knock on every door if we have to."

"Or try the maid," Sophie said.

"That's good. I don't recall her name."

"Bonnie," Sophie said immediately. "Fiftyish, fading red hair, green eyes."

Jack whistled softly. "I have to admit I barely remembered what she looked like."

"That's because you were busy trying to hide your

attempt to break into Sabrina's room. Let's split up and question people. It'll be faster that way."

He smiled as he got to his feet. "Let's just do it together. Maybe one of us will pick up things the other misses."

They started with the valet, who was a different guy from the one who had helped them earlier. As many of the conference attendees were calling for their cars in order to leave the hotel for dinner elsewhere in town, he didn't have time to ponder the photo. Because he hadn't been on duty since the day before, it seemed a moot point. The housekeeper had gone home for the day, and though Jack protested, they split up with Sophie taking the front desk and Jack going down to the basement to try to find the handyman he'd glimpsed when he and Sabrina first went to her room. Maybe he saw or heard something.

"Ask if Sabrina called or has any messages," he told Sophie before he left her side.

"Will do," Sophie said.

Jack was pretty sure the reason he didn't want Sophie out of his sight was because she was his sole link to Sabrina. At least it felt as though she was. No two women could look that much alike and not have very close connections.

The truth was, however, he suspected it also had to do with the fact that he was worried she was in the line of fire that he felt partially responsible for creating.

The basement was a brightly lit network of rooms portioned off for conference seminars and was all but empty now. He made his way to the housekeeping, kitchen and maintenance facilities and found a small room labeled Maintenance.

"Hank Tyson never showed up today," Jack was informed by a harried-looking man wearing a badge proclaiming he was Jerry Able, head of housekeeping. "I'm filling in for him. I don't know how he handles this job all by himself. With the hotel this crowded, the list of complaints is longer than Santa's naughty list."

"I saw someone in coveralls carrying a toolbox up on three a few hours ago," Jack said.

"Wasn't me. I called in a local guy to help out. Had to. With this many guests, we've got dozens of heater failures, clogged sinks, stuck windows, issues with dead bolts—you name it. Brad Withers and the new guy he hired, Adam something, tried to stay on top of everything. You must have seen one of them." He frowned as he added, "Wait, do you have an emergency? What kind?"

"No emergency," Jack said. He called up the picture of the man in the hoodie. "Is this Brad Withers or Adam?"

"I don't know," Jerry said. "I mean it's not Brad for sure but I've never actually seen Adam."

Jack retraced his steps to the lobby, where he found Sophie. He told her the little bit he'd learned. "How about you? Did the desk have any information? Does Sabrina have any messages?"

She shook her head. "Most of the staff has turned over. No one recognized the photo of the man in the hoodie that you sent to my phone. Only one woman remembers Sabrina and that was just because she checked her in this morning. She thought I was her and issued me a new room key. I let it ride."

"We need people to be looking for her," he said.

"Well, it was the only way I could learn anything about messages. I'll go clear it up."

He caught her arm. "Let me think for a minute."

"I thought I could stay in her room tonight," Sophie explained. "If she comes back, I can let you know. Are you on the same floor?"

"I don't have a room here either," he said. "The hotel found me a place a mile or two down the road. It's called Pine Lodge or Pine Lane or something."

"Pine Ledge," she said and shuddered dramatically. "You don't want to stay there."

"I've probably stayed in worse," he said. "As for you in Sabrina's room…are you forgetting she more or less disappeared from there?"

"I haven't forgotten. She must have answered the door to someone who enticed her away—"

"Or snatched her," he said and even he heard the despair in his voice. This could not be happening, not to Buzz and not on Jack's watch. He was the one who insisted she take a nap and then left her alone. Where was she? Was he wasting time staying in this hotel?

"Wait a second," he said aloud. "How did the guy terrorizing Sabrina get a room here if he was just following her? The hotel has been booked for well over a week. He would have had to already have a reservation, which meant he was privy to her plans and that probably means he's someone Sabrina knows."

She looked uneasy, as though a thought had occurred to her that she was reluctant to voice. "Go on, say whatever it is you're thinking," he prompted her.

"Don't they say it's usually the one closest to a person who—"

"No," he interrupted. "Buzz would never hurt Sabrina or engage someone else to do it for him."

"But—"

"No. The man is as good as a brother to me. I know him. I know how he feels about his wife. Whoever is terrorizing Sabrina is breaking into her house, dropping rocks on top of her, following her and, maybe now, stealing her out of her room. No way does Buzz have anything to do with any of this."

"Okay."

He made a sudden decision. "There's a chair in the hall," he announced. "I'm going to park myself in it. I know I won't sleep if I'm three miles away no matter how good or bad the hotel is so I might as well fidget the night away where I can keep an eye on the door to your—her—room."

Sophie stared at him a second. "I've known you for about three hours. You confronted me in the lobby, called me a nutcase, more or less, and then showed me a picture of a woman who looks a lot like me."

"Identical to you. You keep shying away from that."

She waved an impatient hand. "That's not the point. I'm not sure why, but I trust you. If you knew me you'd realize how crazy that is because I'm one of those cautious people who drive the rest of the world to drink. Anyway, stay in Sabrina's room with me. If she does come back in the middle of the night, at least she'll recognize one of us."

"Actually, she'll recognize both of us."

"Are you taking the offer or not?"

"You sure?"

"Positive. I plan on calling room service for dinner. I don't know about you, but I'm hungry and tired and I have a lot of deep thinking to accomplish. You in?"

"Absolutely," he said. "Just let me get my suitcase out of the car. Can I get yours for you?"

"I don't have one," she said. "I believe I may have mentioned I left kind of spontaneously."

"Wait right here," he told her. "I'll be right back."

THEY ATE CHICKEN sandwiches while they watched the local news. It wasn't until it was over that Sophie realized Jack had been waiting for some kind of a horrible report that a female body had been discovered on a lonely beach or at the bottom of a cliff. She was glad she hadn't thought of that.

The room came with two queen-size beds so where to sleep didn't pose an issue. A bigger problem was the fact that Sophie didn't have anything to change into. Jack solved that by handing her his pajama top, which brushed her knees, and then putting on his bottoms.

"I saw this very scenario in one of my mother's old movies," Sophie told him as they stood a few feet apart looking each other over. "I believe it's time for you to string a clothesline between our beds so we can drape a blanket to preserve my modesty."

He laughed, then he sat down on the bed and fooled with the alarm on his phone. She glanced at him again, rather taken aback by all the muscles in his chest and the hypnotizing shape of his well-formed arms. Was he trying to prove something by parading all that male virility so close she could touch—

Wait a second, just stop. Since when had things like rippling muscles and toned abs intimidated her? She wasn't even interested in that kind of thing. A person's mind was the true seat of sensuality.

Really? her subconscious chided. *What about Danny's mind did you find so terribly stimulating?*

That was a tricky one. In fact, she'd be hard-pressed to truly define him. In ways, he'd seemed one faceted, but then again, she'd known him only a few weeks. What he might have lacked in original thought, she decided, he made up for in other endearing qualities. Like the way they always laughed at the same things. Really, they never even disagreed let alone argued.

Until this morning.

In her head, she heard him tell her mother that he found Sophie's enthusiasm about her students and her job "cute."

"Cute" sat heavy in her heart.

"Looks like you're working away on those deep thoughts," Jack said as he checked his phone messages.

"Any word?" she asked, ignoring his remark.

"Just work-related stuff, nothing from Sabrina. So, what were you thinking about?"

"Danny."

He put the phone aside. "Go on. This sounds interesting."

She wished she knew Jack well enough to ask him to put on a T-shirt. His chest with its fine sprinkling of dark hair was distracting. And where did those square shoulders come from? Did he spend half his life in a gym?

Just as though he read her mind—or perhaps her stare—he got up and snatched a forest green T-shirt out of his suitcase, pulled it over his head and returned to his bed. It kind of helped. "You were going to tell me about your Danny," he said with an encouraging smile.

"Not my Danny, not anymore," she said and sat down on the edge of her mattress facing him, making sure their knees didn't touch. They were very close nonetheless, something that might have bothered her more if his comment hadn't driven home the fact that she'd blown it with Danny. He was gone by now, taking her opportunity for marriage and family with him. This hadn't bothered her hours before, but now, as the dark outside the hotel window pressed against the window glass, she suddenly felt adrift.

Instead of telling Jack little or nothing as she had planned, she found herself spilling her guts and, by voicing the events of the morning, reliving them. He didn't say a word as she spoke, and when she was finished she met his gaze. "Do you think I was unfair to him?"

He responded at once. "*You* unfair to *him*? Hardly. I think Danny has to take the heat for this mess. The guy sounds...odd."

She felt a sudden wave of defensiveness for Danny. After all, Jack had heard only her side of the story and as she'd retold it, her own complicity in what happened is what struck her. "I don't know if that's a fair observation," she said.

"Tell me how you met."

She smiled. "It was like a movie in a way, you know, guy trying to figure out what kind of apple to choose, girl—who happened to be a big fan of apples—offering advice. He was very sweet. He explained his company had sent him to Portland for a few weeks and admitted he was lonely. He asked me out to dinner and when I said yes he seemed so pleased. I was craving Italian food. Turns out it was his favorite, too. It was just so—"

"Suspicious?" he said.

She frowned. "Cynic. I thought it was exciting. He asked my opinion about things and listened to my answers—that's a very engaging thing for a guy to do. And he's super kind to my mother. She isn't exactly easy to get along with. She and I—well, we're like oil and water. It would be a war zone if I hadn't learned not to react to every little thing. Anyway, back to Danny. His marriage proposal came with a ready-made honeymoon, a big house one block over for us to live in and financial aid for my mother in the form of live-in help so she can stay in her own house. And he even quit his job with a prestigious law firm up in Seattle to relocate to Portland. That's pretty amazing, right? I don't know why it hit me so hard this morning."

"Then I stand corrected," Jack said. "The guy sounds like a prize. Why *did* you turn him down?"

"It was just so unexpected. And it was hard thinking straight with my mother butting in all the time."

"Why was she there again?"

"She lives with me, or I live with her. It was her and Dad's house and then she lost it after he died. I bought it back when I finished college and started teaching. She has a few health issues that aren't as bad as she thinks they are, but, well, the truth is, she can't afford to live on her own and I can't afford separate housing for her."

"Sounds like you and she have an…uneasy… relationship," he said.

She started to protest but nodded instead. "Yeah, it is. I'm a disappointment."

He looked incredulous. "What?"

She shrugged one shoulder. "I'm not big enough, you know?"

"Physically, you're perfect so what does that mean?"

She fought the moment of pleasure his compliment created. "I'm not smart enough or funny enough or ambitious enough or… You know what I mean. I understand most of her bitterness comes from Dad dying so young and all the burdens of raising a kid falling on her shoulders. He left Mom with few resources."

"Sounds as if you've been trying to make things up to her since then. How old were you when he died?"

"Eleven. He was the one who wanted children. Mom really didn't, she was happy with just the two of them, but he talked her into it. My birth caused all sorts of physical issues for her."

"How do you know all this?"

"She told me."

He stared at her for a long minute, the blue of his eyes filling her whole head. "Sophie, what kind of parent tells their child they didn't want them?"

Sophie blinked. She couldn't think of a word to say.

Out of loyalty at the very least, she should defend her mom, but words just escaped her.

"Does Danny know about this?" Jack asked.

She swallowed and, for the second time that day, that stone-like feeling started to creep up her legs toward her heart. She stood abruptly and glanced longingly at the door. She was running out of safe havens. Taking a deep breath, she slowly sat back down. "I think it's kind of hard to miss," she admitted.

"Then why did he propose in front of her?"

"I wondered that, too. I don't know."

"Why didn't he ask you to step outside?"

She gestured toward the window, through which nothing could be seen. "It was cold and pouring down rain."

"Trust me," he said softly. "If I loved a woman enough to ask her to share the rest of my life and I knew someone intimidated her, I would stand in a blizzard to talk to her in private. The only reason I would do it right there in front of that person—" He stopped short. "Well, what do I know?"

"Finish what you were going to say."

"I've said enough," he mumbled. "Only, if this guy is such a dandy listener, then how did he so totally misread your level of commitment?"

"I must have misled him."

"You seem pretty straightforward to me," he said.

"I'm not myself today," she mumbled.

"Maybe you are yourself today."

"What does that mean?"

"Maybe today you got pushed over your own personal edge of tolerance. Maybe today you finally got tired of never being heard."

Once again his blue gaze filled her vision. She rubbed her forehead until it faded away.

"I'm sorry," Jack said into the continuing silence. His voice turned introspective as he added, "I have no right to counsel anyone on romance and love."

Anxious for a chance to focus the spotlight elsewhere, she perked up. "That's a provocative sentence. Care to explain it?"

"No, I do not." He opened the bed and got under the covers. "I'm ready to put an end to this day. How about you?"

"Please."

She lay there in the dark, very aware of Jack just a few feet away, listening to him breathe. It was a nice, steady, reassuring noise, and as her mind drifted she admitted that although his comments and questions had been probing and painful, she'd enjoyed talking to him. Was there any truth in what he said?

Eventually her thoughts circled back to Danny and she recalled the times she'd basked in his compliments. Now, in retrospect, she'd been like a thirsty flower aching for water. She sometimes found children like this in her classroom and her heart always went out to them. Was that partially because she recognized their need in herself?

Man, that was embarrassing but she could feel the truth lurking in there somewhere. If Danny had seen her only as an easy way to fill a few idle hours, then why quit his job and move, why buy a house, why ask her to marry him?

What if he truly did love her? What if he'd just gotten heavy-handed with the marriage stuff and just wanted to share the moment with her mother, who, face it, was an awfully big part of Sophie's life. She knew he'd tried to call several times today, she'd seen his name on her screen every time she looked... What if she'd just told him she needed a few days to think instead of running away? What if she'd had a backbone and insisted she and Danny go talk in the kitchen? Why was it his problem to figure out her needs?

What had she done?

If she'd been alone in the room, she would have switched on the light, gotten dressed and driven home. She suddenly had no idea what she was doing here.

And then she remembered Sabrina. Sabrina, missing. Sabrina absent from this room without explanation, drawn by someone or something she couldn't ignore. Sophie knew in a moment of insight only two things could do that. Love...or fear. Jack was adamant that his friend would not be behind anything that would harm Sabrina, and she would have to accept he knew what he was talking about. But what if Sabrina had called her husband for comfort? Maybe Buzz knew where she'd gone.

Fear was different. Fear could be generated by something hidden, something Sabrina might not have confessed to her husband or his best friend, a secret, something that caught up with her.

Regardless of anything else, where was Sabrina

right now? Sophie fell asleep saying a silent prayer that wherever she was it was because she wanted to be there and she was safe.

It was impossible to tell how much time had elapsed when a voice woke her from her sleep. She sat up immediately, her heart in her throat, and scanned the room. "Sabrina?" she said and was met by nothing but silence. A line of light shone under the door but the rest of the room was dark and still. And then she heard the voice again, and realized it came from Jack.

"Lisa," he moaned, and then, "No!" uttered with a gut-wrenching sob that sent chills washing through Sophie's body.

"No, no," he whispered again, pain dripping from his voice like blood from a wounded animal.

Sophie lay frozen, not sure what to do. As the sound of tossing and turning continued, she slipped out of bed and approached his dark shape. He was mumbling now, his head turning from side to side. She sat down beside him and he immediately clutched her wrist.

"It's okay," she said in a calm voice. "Everything's fine. You're safe."

His grip didn't loosen and his body stayed rigid. She had the feeling he was like a soldier in a trench, lying in wait, uncertain what was coming but geared up to annihilate it in order to stay alive.

She tried to reach the light switch on the lamp but it was just out of reach. The shifting of her body weight made his grip tighten.

"Jack," she said. "It's me, Sophie, remember? We

met earlier today, here in Seaport. I'm the girl with the purple streak in my hair."

For the first time, his fingers relaxed, but he still didn't let go. She took a deep breath and continued prattling on about nothing as she adjusted herself on the bed next to him, propped up on his spare pillow, half sitting with her legs stretched out in front of her. She stroked his hair without considering whether or not it was too personal. He was in pain, that much was clear.

When his restlessness stopped and his breathing returned to normal, she slowly withdrew her hand, but when she shifted her weight to stand, his arm slipped over her legs and his head fell against her hip. Trapped!

But not uncomfortable.

She tugged on a corner of the blanket to get a little coverage, then settled down, her intention to wait until he started snoring and then disengage herself. It seemed like second nature to continue stroking his fine hair as she leaned back and closed her eyes.

Who was Lisa and what in the world had happened to her?

Chapter Four

Jack awoke without the help of his phone alarm. He always did and wasn't even sure why he still bothered to set it except for some superstitious feeling that if he didn't, that would be the one time his internal alarm took a hike.

As he became aware that sunlight actually peeked through the gap in the drapes, he also figured out his pillow was the lap of the woman slumped in bed beside him.

He recalled Sophie's coming to him last night. He'd had a nightmare about Lisa, one so real the dream had crossed into reality. He could remember holding Sophie's hand very tight to keep from slipping back into the void. Her voice had been like a lantern in a lighthouse illuminating a path back to safety. He'd wanted her to keep talking forever.

He hoisted himself up on one elbow and looked at her. A lock of purple hair fell over her right eye. In repose, she looked impossibly young, and when he thought back to the things she'd revealed about her boyfriend and her mother, the very people who seemed to form the core of her support system, he felt anger pump in his veins.

As he watched, she scrunched up her nose and yawned and then her eyes flew open.

"Good morning," he said.

"Hmm—"

"Looks like we have a break in the rain."

"Oh, Lord," she groaned. "Save me from morning people."

Her voice brought him firmly back to the here and now. He scooted off the bed and grabbed his phone, hoping against hope that there would be a message from Sabrina. Sophie's sudden stillness announced her awareness of this possibility, as well. He shook his head. "Not a word. That's it. I'm driving to Astoria."

"That's where she lives."

"It is. I can't sit around here anymore. Probably should have left last night."

She popped to her feet. "I'll take the first shower," she said. "I take short ones. Saves water, you know. That'll give me a chance to dry my hair while you take yours."

"I think—"

"You're not going to argue about this, are you?" she interrupted. "Look, I'll follow your car in mine unless you want to try to go without me, in which case I'll find my own way."

"I'll order breakfast," he said. He hadn't intended to talk her out of it. Instead, he'd been about to agree that until they identified this bozo intent on harming Sabrina, Sophie should stay where he could protect her, but there really wasn't any point in saying that now. Nor would he mention his gut feeling that his, Sophie's and Sabrina's destinies were all tied together in some cosmic knot.

He made the rest of his usual calls—Sabrina's house to leave yet another message on the land phone they still kept for emergencies; the police who had nothing to report; the local hospital; the front desk; valet parking. Nothing. The woman was just flat out not here.

Sophie came back in the room five minutes later, still wearing his pajama top, her hair wrapped up in a towel. He tore his gaze away from her shapely bare legs and her very pretty heart-shaped face. How that very face on Sabrina could seem remote and collected and yet look so vivid and irresistible on Sophie was a mystery to him.

"Breakfast is on the way," he said, and strode past her into the bathroom, a change of clothes in his hands. He turned at the door. "Everything in my suitcase will swim on you but you're welcome to borrow what you need."

SOPHIE SPENT SEVERAL minutes blow-drying her new hair. She loved the darker brown; finally the shade enhanced her skin. She loved the chic bounce of the shorter cut and the new longish bangs. It was the purple streak that jumped out at her but she could recall telling the hairdresser to do what she wanted, just as long as it was different. She couldn't deny the woman's panache and Sophie had to admit that life had certainly gotten more interesting since making the change.

Last night, she'd felt trapped in a web of her own making, a web created by the endless second-guessing that inevitably occurred as a postscript to any act of defiance no matter how small or even justified. Equilibrium had returned with the light of day, and this morning when she thought of going back to Danny it was to apologize for bolting, to return his ring and offer support as he figured out what to do about a honeymoon they wouldn't take, a house they wouldn't live in and a job he'd quit on what had to be a whim.

But right now, Sabrina came first. Where was she?

A knock on the door sounded at the same time the water went off in the bathroom. Sophie stood between the two doors, half-dressed. She ran to the door but without opening hollered, "Yes?"

"Room service."

"Please leave the tray," she said, and ran back to the pile of clothes on a chair to pull on yesterday's leggings and T-shirt before Jack caught her seminude. His open suitcase beckoned her. She looked through his neatly folded belongings until her fingers grazed the cloud-soft fibers of cashmere. She pulled out a sweater the color of a summer sky and tugged it over her head, where it slid down her body to midthigh. Cozy but oversize on her, she bet it molded Jack's arms and torso and highlighted his eyes. This was the kind of sweater a woman might buy for her lover, and with that thought, last night's anguished call for Lisa rang in her ears.

Could she ask him about her? No, she decided. A cry in the night was not an open invitation to pry.

The bathroom door opened and a freshly showered Jack stood framed in the doorway for an instant.

"That sweater looks great on you," he said as he walked back into the room. His own clothes consisted of black boots, gray pants and a charcoal sweater. Damp, black hair curled around his ears. He looked urbane and pulled together and yet now that she knew him a little better, totally approachable.

"Thanks," she said. "I have an idea."

"What's that?"

"I got to thinking that maybe Sabrina called Buzz after you left her to rest. Maybe she realized she needed to be with him. Maybe she left on the run to drive back to Portland to catch a flight—"

"Wait a second," he said. "Slow down. Getting to Antarctica isn't a piece of cake. There are no direct flights. It takes some planning."

"But it could be done."

"Maybe. The airport is three hours from here, though. In all that time she couldn't stop and contact me or answer one of my calls?"

"There may be a reason. Cell phones run out of battery or break." She studied her feet for a second before adding, "I just realized that I've done the same thing."

"In what way?"

"I left without explanation, although people did see me drive away. I came to the coast without telling anyone where I was going, I'm not registered at any hotel and I haven't answered my phone even once. The people in my life are just as clueless about me as we are about Sabrina."

"You need to call your mother or Danny."

"I know. I will. I've been so wrapped up in myself that it didn't even cross my mind until now. Does that give us hope about Sabrina just wandering off for some reason and not thinking to call?"

"The situation, as far as I know, isn't quite the same. She elicited my help. I don't think she'd leave me hanging. I'm not saying it couldn't happen, it just seems unlikely. And I'm not discounting how much she must have wanted to run to Buzz, but he's currently aboard a Russian ship with a bunch of other scientists from all over the world visiting islands no one else ever goes to. Right now getting to him is a pretty daunting task."

Sophie took a deep breath. "Don't take this the wrong way but is it possible you said something to her yesterday that would cause her to cut you out of the loop?"

If someone had asked her that question, she knew she would have immediately replayed every word she'd uttered the day before, but Jack just shook his head.

Such confidence!

"But you make a good point. Yesterday she was adamant about protecting Buzz but she may have changed her mind. It's possible she contacted him. I'll think of some way to find out if he's heard from her. But we also need to talk to her coworkers. She said they were like family. Maybe she ran to one of them for help." He looked down at Sophie and smiled. "I'm sorry I jumped on your idea when you first broached it. I shouldn't have interrupted you."

Her hand landed on his arm and once again she got

that tingly feeling, but this time she knew it had nothing to do with his clothes. It was just him, plain and simple. He probably affected everyone this way. "It's no big deal," she said. "We're both on edge."

He glanced at her hand before meeting her gaze. Something passed between them; Sophie had no idea what. She removed her hand while struggling to think of something to say. He took care of it. "I was hoping the coffee got here. I hate the stuff you make in the room."

She tore her attention away from him, not an easy feat. "It did come," she said. "It's in the hall."

"I'll get it," he told her and broke the connection that had fused them together for a few seconds by striding to the door. She cleared the table.

"Have a seat if you're hungry," he said as he kicked the door closed behind him and carried the lidded tray into the room. "I also ordered bacon and eggs for two."

"Sounds wonderful," she said, claiming one of the chairs. As he set the lid aside, she reached to pour the coffee, then paused as she glanced at the plates of goodies.

"What's wrong?" he asked.

She smiled up at him as she set aside the coffee thermos. "What's that perched beside the salt and pepper? It's so cute." She lowered her fingers.

Jack grabbed her hand. "Don't touch it," he cautioned.

"Why not? Maybe the hotel—"

"The hotel had nothing to do with this," he interrupted, leaning down to look at the little folded figurine.

"Then who did?" she asked.

"I believe we can thank the guy you recognized in the photo."

"The one you think has Sabrina?"

"Not anymore I don't," he said, peering closely at the tray. "Sabrina received a couple of foxes folded out of dollar bills just like this one when she was up in Astoria. Another one showed up on her breakfast tray yesterday morning, sixty miles south of here and following the falling rock incident."

"Odd."

"If the man who is planting them took her or enticed her away, he'd know she wasn't in this room. For that matter, if it's the same guy he'd also know she wasn't in the garage last night. That means he thinks you're Sabrina, which means he doesn't know she's missing, which probably means she isn't missing at all, she's just gone off somewhere and, like you said, something happened to her phone."

"That's good news, right?" Sophie asked.

"I think so." He opened his pocketknife to a pair of tweezers. "Will you please get me one of those plastic sleeves they wrap around the water glasses?" he said as he removed the fox from the tray.

"Fingerprints?" she asked as he slid it into the plastic she fetched. He nodded. "Why would this cute little thing frighten Sabrina?" she asked.

Jack took the plastic from her and tucked it in his suitcase. When he turned back to her, his expression was thoughtful. "She received two or three of these before she left Astoria, all anonymously. And now they're following her on her vacation. It's not the fox that's frightening, it's the intent behind it. Someone thumbing their nose at her, saying, 'I can get to you whenever I want. I'm watching you.'"

"But why fold it out of a dollar bill?"

"I don't know. How long ago did the tray arrive?"

"It came to the door right as you turned off the shower."

"Ten, fifteen minutes," he said. "That means that whoever is stalking Sabrina Long Cromwell stood outside that door waiting for an opportunity to interact with her. The tray being left must have made his day."

She looked from his gaze to the bounty of untouched food. "I don't think I can eat any of that," she said.

"Me neither, but you've started me thinking like a detective again. See if you can find more of the plastic bags. I'll take a sample of everything on that tray and have it analyzed to see if whoever is taunting her with folded money is also trying to poison her. While I do that, why don't you call down for another tray. This time we'll leave the door open."

THE EMPLOYEE WHO delivered the second tray now took away the first. Before he left, Jack showed him the photo of the hooded guy on his phone, but the kid denied ever seeing the man and knew nothing about what happened after he left the tray in the hall.

After picking at their new breakfast, Sophie turned on her phone. "Better get this over with," she said with a glance at Jack, and he could feel her stress level rise. "Mom, hi, it's me," she finally said.

Jack glanced at her face as she obviously listened to her mother. She frowned at last and seemed to measure her words. "I know I'm lucky," she said. "I know he's a great catch."

She listened some more and he found himself feeling fidgety on her behalf.

"Wait, what?" After a few seconds, she took a deep breath. "I don't know. Maybe, I have to think about it… Yeah, I'm crazy, I get it. Listen, I'll be home tonight sometime…No, please don't call Danny. I just didn't want you to worry."

She listened again, her expression now impatient. "Well, I guess it's good I'm so predictable, isn't it?" she finally said and ended the call.

She looked at him immediately and he smiled.

"Feel better?" he asked her.

"No. Let's get out of here."

"Do you want to talk?"

"No," she said. "Last night the desk clerk said Sabrina is booked through Tuesday."

Sophie obviously wanted to get back to business. "Then we won't check her out of the hotel," Jack said after a moment's thought. It was kind of hard to picture her coming back here but if she didn't, what did that say, that she wasn't able to return, that she wasn't able to answer his calls or respond to his messages? There were only three reasons that could be true. She was off on some secret mission, so to speak; she was injured and her situation precluded contacting someone; or she'd been abducted and denied the opportunity.

Face it. Option three was what terrified him. Three was his Lisa.

He stowed his suitcase in his car, then he and Sophie went downstairs to show the photo of the guy in the hoodie to anyone who would stop long enough to look. At the front desk, they asked about the woman who opened their room for them, Bonnie, and was told today was her day off.

Jack wondered if he should get a last name and look her up for questioning and decided to give the information he had to Sergeant Jones at the police station. Let him do the follow-up; Jack was anxious to get to Astoria. A man who usually operated on logic, he found himself being ruled by his gut and his gut said, hit the road.

"How 'bout your maintenance guy, Hank? Is he around today?"

"He didn't show up again. Jerry's still covering for him."

"What about the local guys Jerry called in? Is one of them around?"

"Brad Withers is in the basement. You can catch him there if you hurry," the clerk told them before turning her attention to a tagged conference official who was having trouble with an overhead projector.

They found Withers in an anteroom in the basement digging through a pile of stuff in the corner. He glanced over his shoulder when he heard them in the doorway. His round bald head reflected what little light the overhead bulb produced. Jack had never seen anyone so hairless. Even his eyelashes looked translucent, like the fins of some tiny fish. He sure as heck wasn't the guy Jack had seen upstairs the day before; that must have been the other one.

"You folks need something?" he asked. "Call the desk and tell them. I'll get to you when I can."

Jack flicked on his phone and showed Brad the photo of the guy in the hooded sweatshirt. "Do you recognize him?" he asked.

"Sure, I seen him," Brad said. "Up on three, I think. Yesterday morning, late. Me and Adam were working on a heater unit up there. Adam left to drive into town to hunt down a part. I got bored and wandered out in the hall to sneak a smoke. This guy was standing by the elevator." He turned back to the dark corner. "Turn your phone this way. The light is helping. Lower." He made a triumphant sound. "There's the pipe wrench, right in front of my nose."

"Do you know the guy's name?" Sophie asked.

Brad stuffed the wrench in a bucket with some other tools. "Nope. Ask Bonnie."

"She's off today," Jack said.

"Nah, she's up on three again covering for someone with a sick kid."

"But the front desk—"

"Trust me," Brad interrupted.

Jack and Sophie exchanged quick glances and took off. They found Bonnie just coming out of a room. "You lock yourself out again?" she asked as she caught sight of Sophie.

"Not this time. Would you look at a photo for us?"

Jack pulled out his phone. Bonnie peered at the screen and huffed. "That's Gerald Duff in 308."

"You've met him?" Sophie asked, her voice tinged with excitement.

"Not really but I came up here yesterday to exchange a coffeepot he claimed was broken. He wasn't in the room so I left the new one on the desk right next to a stack of crisp dollar bills. Lot of good it did me."

"What do you mean?" Jack asked.

"He checked out a while ago. It's a holiday tomorrow and that means more people will check in when this group leaves, so I've already cleaned the room and what with the mess he left, I expected a decent tip. This is what I got instead." She dug in her apron pocket and extracted a folded dollar bill. "What do I need a paper dog for?"

"It's a fox," Sophie murmured.

"I don't care what it is," Bonnie declared and shoved it back in her pocket. "Bottom line it's a buck tip for a two-hundred-dollar room. Tightwad."

As she turned to roll her cart down the hall, Jack posed another question. "One more thing. The hotel seems to have been booked solid for the weekend. That means Duff had to have made a reservation, doesn't it?"

She shook her head. "He walked in right after we got a cancellation. I remember because I had to go up to 308 to remove a fruit basket someone had sent for the people who canceled. I bet they would have left a decent tip."

They thanked her for her help and went back to the

desk, where the clerk refused to confirm or deny their former guest's name. Jack called the police and gave them the information, which also gave him a chance to remind Sergeant Jones to keep looking for Sabrina.

"Turns out my wife hates red roses," the sergeant said before hanging up. Jack relayed this information to Sophie, who laughed.

Jack felt a huge wave of relief when they finally drove out of Seaport. He decided at once that the trip would be easier if the rain hadn't started again and more interesting if Sophie was in the car with him. As it was, he'd given her the address and now followed her red compact while keeping an eye out for white sedans with murderous drivers. What he discovered was that there were a lot of white cars.

He couldn't get over Duff leaving the origami fox for the maid. Talk about calling attention to himself! He had to be an idiot or incredibly smug…maybe both. With any luck the police would haul him in for questioning. If they didn't and he was following Sophie right now, her driving up to Sabrina's residence would reinforce his belief that Sophie truly was Sabrina.

Jack's thoughts drifted to Sophie's phone conversation with her mother, especially the comments that seemed to concern Danny. She'd said he'd quit his job in Seattle and accepted a new one in Portland. That meant he would have to take and pass a new bar exam. Would he really quit a good job in Washington before making sure he could practice law in Oregon? Something sounded kind of fishy about it.

Jack could understand how a guy in a new city

would latch onto a pretty companion, especially some-one as warm as Sophie. He could understand how a man would be drawn to her quirky insecurities and ask her to marry him. Unfortunately, the same quirky insecurities that made her lovable also made her vul-nerable. If the guy wasn't head over heels in love with her, then what was his angle?

Jack searched his memory for a second and then realized Sophie hadn't said whether or not she loved Danny, and even if she didn't, he knew people drifted into marriage for lots of reasons and only one of them was love.

And what about that phone call? She'd told her mom she had to think about something. Think about what? Danny? Was the guy still hanging around?

Regardless, on a strictly professional level, he was curious. He wanted to meet Danny, size him up. He hoped this desire stemmed solely from wholesome con-cern and not some irrational spark of jealousy but had to admit he wouldn't bet his life on it.

It was almost noon when they drove into Astoria, Oregon's northernmost coastal town, built where the Pacific Ocean meets the Columbia River. It was a city with a long maritime history, and Jack always enjoyed coming here despite the rain and fog. Sophie seemed to know her way around and it wasn't long before she pulled into a small subdivision in the making.

Up and down the street, still-unbought lots featured small signs with build-to-suit information while a half a dozen complete houses stood on their parcels of land surrounded by relatively new lawns and vegetation.

Those residences all included rocked-in cement pillars housing mailboxes at the end of their driveways. When the subdivision was complete, it would look attractive and uniform, making up in civility what it lacked in originality. It looked like the kind of place young families started.

A smattering of vehicles parked in driveways signified people enjoying the long weekend by staying inside out of the rain. The distinct exception was the Cromwell house, whose driveway was empty. Buzz's rusty SUV was not parked outside, which meant Sabrina was not inside armed with a plausible explanation of what she'd been up to.

He pulled in beside Sophie's car and stared at the dark windows of the neat, well-cared-for craftsman-style house that Buzz and Sabrina had bought nine months before. Only the brightly burning front porch light challenged the gloom.

They both got out of their cars and hurried to the protection of the porch.

"I don't think she's here," Sophie said, her voice reflecting his own disappointment. A tabby cat suddenly jumped onto the back of a chair and stared at them through the window. Sophie put her hand against the glass and the cat carried on as though it had been abandoned for months.

"You've got a friend," Jack said.

"He looks a lot like my cat, Oscar."

"*Her* name is Gabby," Jack said. "She's Sabrina's cat. Buzz complains that she won't give anyone else the time of day."

They both watched as the cat rubbed the glass where Sophie's fingers still lingered. "Kitty doesn't seem the standoffish type," Sophie said.

"Not to you." He opened the screen door and tried the knob. This sent the cat flying. A moment later, they heard her scratching the other side of the wood door as if trying to let them in.

"Too bad Gabby doesn't have opposable thumbs," Sophie said. "Now what?"

He scanned the street, checking for loitering white sedans. "I have a lock-pick set in my glove compartment. It's time to break in."

Chapter Five

It took Jack less than thirty seconds to open the lock on the back door. "Well, that's an eye-opener," Sophie said. "Is it always that easy?"

"Not always. They need to install better locks." He held the door open. Sophie stepped inside as a blur of gray and black stripes escaped to the outside.

"I hope she's not strictly an indoor cat," Sophie said. The tabby had already jumped to the top of the fence and disappeared.

"I'm not sure if she is or not," Jack said.

The kitchen they entered was small but tidy and it looked like it would be filled with sunlight if it ever stopped raining. Jack walked to the window over the sink and peered outside.

"What are you looking at?" she asked as she stood by his side.

"The neighbor's porch. Sabrina said they hired someone to paint it. Does it look painted to you?"

"It's hard to tell through all the rain."

"Still, it's an odd time of year to paint, don't you think?"

He walked out of the kitchen without waiting for an answer. He'd gotten cryptic since entering the house and Sophie didn't blame him. Sabrina missing from a hotel room had been one thing, but Sabrina missing from this house was a whole other matter. The cat anxious for her return, a lacy red sweater on the back of a chair, rubber rain boots lined up neatly by the door, a clean coffee mug in the strainer—it was as though Sabrina might have left this room five minutes before. Missing from this house seemed like missing from her life and while Sophie had been concerned for the woman's safety before, she now found anxiety tying her stomach in tight knots.

She followed Jack into what turned out to be the living area, which was one big room full of wood walls and shelves, earth-colored furniture, family photographs and large paintings all depicting local scenic scenes. While Jack searched the house—for uninvited guests, she assumed—Sophie's attention was drawn to a grouping of wood-framed photographs displayed on the wall above a low bookcase.

All together there were ten photos that appeared to capture a life in progression. The first one was taken of a very pretty smiling woman standing on a beach, a swaddled baby in her arms. From there, the pictures included various people but the focus was always on the same child who grew older from shot to shot. Preschool, birthdays, graduations…it was all there. The last photo was of three people who sat side by side on a log. The woman was the same as the one in the first picture only two decades older. A college-age girl sat in the middle with a middle-aged man on her left side.

The girl was Sophie only it wasn't.

"Is it like looking at your own family photos?" Jack asked from beside her.

"More like seeing yourself in an alternate universe," Sophie said softly. "Are these Sabrina's parents?"

"Yeah."

"This last picture can't be more than six or seven years old. Her parents are pretty young. Do they live locally?"

"They're both dead," Jack said. "Sabrina said they were trapped in a house fire about six months after that photo was taken."

"Is that why she became—"

"A firefighter? Probably. I know something like that led to my becoming a cop."

"Lisa," Sophie said, and wished immediately she hadn't allowed the word to slip through her lips.

He took a step back as though she'd punched him in the gut.

"I'm sorry, Jack. I shouldn't have mentioned her name. I don't know why I made the leap to you becoming a cop..."

"It's okay," he said. "It's been ten years and she's acutely responsible for what I've become. Not by design on her part, I can assure you. Don't worry, I'm not going to lose it. Nightmares about her have tapered off dramatically over the years. I don't know why they've returned. Anyway, did you look like Sabrina when you were a kid?"

"According to my dad's photographs, almost exactly. My hair was longer. That's about it. I wish I understood how that's possible." As she spoke, she looked around the room. It was easy to appreciate the woodsy casualness of the interior. When the fireplace was lit, she bet the small love seat pulled up in front of it would provide a cozy spot to cuddle with a special someone. Almost as though she felt the other woman's emotions, she was suddenly washed with a feeling of loneliness.

"Sabrina really misses her husband. I hope he comes home soon."

Jack didn't question how she could say such a thing. "I know she misses him. But right now the main priority is finding her."

"And how do we do that?"

"First we call our old friend Sergeant Jones of the Seaport police and see if he's tracked down Gerald Duff." He took out his phone and walked back into the kitchen. Sophie heard his voice ask for the sergeant. He was frowning when he reentered the room a few minutes later.

"Well?"

"The bad news is that Gerald Duff is a stolen identity. They tried dusting his room for prints, but as we know, it had already been cleaned. The plate number he left is also false. The good news is that they're taking Sabrina's disappearance more seriously. They're sending an officer over here to collect the food samples we took from the breakfast tray."

"It sounds as if they're narrowing their search to

the guy I saw in the hall. I don't think he even knows
Sabrina is missing."

"Because he thinks you're her. I agree."

"Did you explain?"

"Yeah, but they're going to go about this their own
way. And in the end, who knows how much this guy
saw? He may not be responsible for Sabrina's disappearance, but if he was stalking her, he might have seen
something that would indicate who is. Plus if they get
him off the street, it'll be safer for you."

"What do we do in the meantime?"

"Conduct our own investigation. I'm going to tackle
Buzz's desk computer. It's time to contact him. Sabrina's
been gone for almost twenty-four hours. There isn't a
doubt in my mind that something has happened to her."

"Mine either," Sophie said.

"How about you look through the drawers and see
if you find anything that sheds light on this situation."

"Okay."

They stared at each other for a long second, then
Jack closed the distance between them and gently put
his arms around her. For a moment, Sophie froze, but
then she slowly melted against his chest. He held her
very tight. If she'd been cold, his embrace would have
suffused her with warmth. What she gathered from
him now was more than warmth—it was courage that
flushed through her body, and hope.

As comforting as this was, his arms also sparked
awareness she'd so far refused to examine. When he
drew back to look down at her, she met his gaze, struggling to understand what was happening. He was a

strong, gorgeous, kind man and she liked him, trusted him, cared what he thought.

But honesty bit at her heart. She more than liked and trusted him. It wasn't just that she enjoyed his company—she yearned for it.

"You okay?" he asked as he released his grip on her arms.

"I think this house is getting to me."

"I know. It's so…empty. I'm going out to the car to get those samples for the police. Let's find out what we need to and get out of here."

Sophie nodded and escaped into the bedroom.

EVENTUALLY THE POLICE came and collected the food samples and the origami fox they'd found on their breakfast tray. They related to Sophie and Jack that a search had been launched to find Sabrina's car and, hence, establish her whereabouts. Sophie wasn't sure what Jack thought of their assurances; she only knew they didn't help her a lot. If she stepped back and looked at the situation honestly, however, she wasn't sure what else they could do. The man she thought of as Gerald Duff was still their only lead.

Meanwhile, Sophie found a cat box, food and water dispensers for the cat. That might mean Gabby was a house cat or it might just mean Sabrina kept her in when she traveled. At any rate, Sophie went to the kitchen door and called for the cat, but she didn't appear.

By the time deep shadows fell over the house, Sophie had found bits and pieces of paper scattered around Sabrina's desk computer. Lists, notes on hotel reservations, doodles, scribbled telephone numbers with a single name to identify them…nothing of import until she opened a drawer to reveal a duo of origami foxes tucked in the corner. Looking at the tiny folded dollar bills gave Sophie the willies and she could not imagine why she had ever thought them cute.

As she put everything back in a small closet that had yielded zero information, Jack appeared in the doorway. "She has a computer, too?" he said, and immediately sat down at the desk. "If I can get into her bank account I can find out if she's using her credit cards. Look around for phone information so we can conduct a search on her calls. If she's using her phone, it probably means she's okay."

As they worked, she asked him if he reached Buzz.

"I tried to call him, but that didn't work," he said, and her heart went out to him. In her gut she knew that his distress over Sabrina tied into whatever had happened to Lisa all those years before. She could see it in his eyes and hear it in his voice. And in this scenario, Buzz was Jack.

"To tell you the truth, I'm not positive what time it is there. I think it's twenty hours ahead of us. Since it's four o'clock here that makes it about noon tomorrow there. Anyway, I sent him an email."

"What did you tell him?" she asked as she found a folder labeled Northwoods Credit Union and handed it to Jack.

"Everything," he said. "If she were my wife, I'd want to know. He deserves the truth."

"I can't find anything about her phone," she said as Jack typed in the credit union information. "I did find her planner, though. She has several notes about favorite coworkers. You know, meeting Sue for lunch or going hiking with someone named Kyle."

"Kyle?" he said, brows furled.

Kyle Woods. She smiled. "Don't get all excited. Just because a woman mentions a man doesn't mean she's romantically involved with him."

"I know that but if Sabrina was involved with this Kyle guy it could explain why she disappeared without a word and why she didn't want Buzz to know. Maybe Kyle's girlfriend or wife is behind the foxes. Or maybe Sabrina tried to break it off and—"

"Slow down," Sophie said, mimicking the advice he'd given her that morning, and yet she remembered thinking herself that harboring a secret could compel a person to vanish. She felt strongly that this wasn't the case with Sabrina, at least as far as a boyfriend was concerned, but that was just her gut speaking and her gut didn't have that great a track record. "The guy behind the origami is a man, not a woman," she said.

"Well, you see, we don't really know that, do we?"

"I still think you're stretching."

"I know I'm stretching but people will be people and we all make bad choices occasionally. Okay, I'll get off that tangent for now but trust me, if I thought of it so will the police and they won't be shy about asking questions." He clicked off the computer and stood. "It doesn't look like she's used her credit card since paying for breakfast yesterday morning. There's no way of knowing if that's good or bad. I think we need to go to the fire station and talk to Sue and Kyle."

"Agreed," she said, anxious to leave the house.

As they passed through the kitchen, Jack glanced out the window. "The neighbor's lights are on. I'm going to go take a peek at the porch and ask a question or two."

"I'll go with you," she said.

But once outside, Sophie glimpsed the tabby walking along the top of the fence. A man in the yard next door was apparently taking the break in the rain to bring in firewood. He carried a load in his arms, but managed to free a hand to wave at her. With a start, Sophie realized he probably thought she was Sabrina and she waved back. "I'll catch up," she told Jack and walked toward the cat, calling, "Kitty, kitty."

The neighbor yelled, "Have you heard from Buzz lately?"

"No," she said as the cat jumped into the yard and started toward Sophie.

The man dumped the wood into a wheelbarrow. The resulting clatter spooked the cat, who turned on a dime and darted around the house toward the street.

Sophie followed at a run. She could not be responsible for losing Sabrina's cat, she just couldn't. She reached the front yard as the cat reached the far sidewalk and trotted onto the muddy driveway of the house under construction. Sophie finally caught up with the tabby when the little rascal stopped to wash her tummy. "Gotcha," she said, and swept her up. The cat immediately went into limp mode and started purring.

"Now you're all friendly?" Sophie said as she hugged the tabby in her arms and started back to the house. As she stepped off the curb, a white car suddenly appeared from a side street. A moment of déjà vu assaulted Sophie's nerves and she stopped dead in her tracks to steel herself for another incident like the one in the garage. This car, however, slowed down as it drew closer, and the passenger window lowered.

Another neighbor mistaking her for Sabrina, she thought, until she found herself facing the barrel of a gun.

JACK WALKED ACROSS the wet grass toward the house on the east side of Buzz and Sabrina's place. The only part of the house visible from their window had been the porch, but as Jack approached he could see the house itself was older and smaller than the new ones springing up in the subdivision surrounding it. No doubt it had once sat on this small plateau more or less by itself.

He was looking for a path around the porch when a sliding glass door opened and a pleasant-looking woman in her forties stepped outside. "I saw you coming from Sabrina's house. Is everything okay over there?"

"Why do you ask?" Jack asked, suddenly alert.

"I just haven't seen her around for a few days. I got worried, you know, what with her husband off on that job and everything."

"She decided to take a little trip," he said.

"Down the coast like she does every year?" the

woman asked, but it was more a statement. "That girl is amazing. Who else goes hiking in February?"

"No one," he said with a laugh. "My name is Jack. Buzz and I go way back. Sabrina mentioned that you had your porch painted recently and I was hoping you could give me the name of the guy you hired."

Her expression turned quizzical. "My porch?" She gestured at the faded paint. "This porch? When? Did she say?"

"About a month ago. She just happened to see a painter over here. Maybe your husband hired someone."

"Tom? Not likely."

They both peered at the protected walls of the inset porch. The only new paint consisted of a couple of whitish brush strokes that stood out against the beige paint. Jack turned to look at Sabrina and Buzz's house and found his gaze centered on the kitchen window.

A couple of Sabrina's statements lingered in his mind. *I was at the kitchen window draining pasta when I thought I saw the painter taking photos of me... I just had the strangest feeling he'd been doing more than taking pictures...*

A decade-old image of Lisa cooking pasta for a photographer flashed in his head. She'd survived the photo shoot but soon after—

Where was Sabrina? For that matter, where was Sophie?

"We didn't hire a painter," the woman was saying. "I have no idea—"

"I must have misunderstood Sabrina," Jack interrupted as he turned on his heels and began retracing his steps. The back of Buzz's house looked deserted. He broke into a jog and headed to the front yard, stopping short when he spied Sophie standing in the street, facing his direction, holding the wiggling cat. A car had stopped between him and her and for a second he thought she was arguing with the driver because even from a distance, he detected waves of tension.

He continued moving, wondering if he dared take time to open the trunk and retrieve his gun. It appeared the driver's attention was on Sophie and not him. However, the late-afternoon light made seeing anything inside the car iffy at best.

And then suddenly it looked like Sophie tossed the cat right at the driver. An explosion sounded and the car spurted forward as though the driver's foot reflexively hit the accelerator pedal.

Sophie took off at a run as the cat came flying back out the window. The car crashed into the construction's trash bin that fell over with a bang, spilling its contents into the street. The driver overcorrected and his car came damn close to hitting Jack, who jumped out of the way as the vehicle continued careening until it smashed into one of the cement pillars holding a mailbox. Jack ran toward the stalled car, but the driver got it going again before he could get there and this time backed up and accelerated like a race-car driver, speeding off down the street until lurching around the corner and roaring out of sight.

Jack looked around for Sophie and found her kneeling by the supine cat. He sprinted over to join her.

"I killed Sabrina's cat!" she said as she lifted the little animal from the pavement and clutched it to her chest.

He looked down at the cat, who was already beginning to squirm in her grasp. "No, she's not dead. See, she's breathing." The cat continued to struggle against Sophie's hands as Jack helped her stand.

"Did he shoot her?" Sophie demanded.

"There's no blood, at least not hers," Jack said as he lifted the angry tabby out of Sophie's grasp to save her from further scratches.

"We have to take her to Dr. London."

"Who?"

"Sabrina's veterinarian. He's on Hyde Street. I saw an invoice for him in Sabrina's papers."

"The cat seems fine," Jack protested. "How about you?"

"I'm okay."

"Did you get a look at him?" Jack asked but he knew the answer, for he had also seen the guy through the windshield and knew he'd hidden his face.

"He had one of the ski mask things on," she said. This conversation was held as they hurried back toward Jack's car. Sophie got into the passenger seat and held out her hands to accept the increasingly irate cat, who now growled and hissed her displeasure. Jack wished he had a box in which to contain the eight pounds of striped fury, but he didn't and it was obvious Sophie was determined to see this through.

"I have to lock their door," he shouted as he ran back

around the house and did just that. They arrived at the vet's a little bloodied but in one piece.

THE RECEPTIONIST ASSUMED Sophie was Sabrina. "Love your hair," she said. "Man, Gabby is going nuts. Let me get you a cat carrier."

Sophie explained about the fall and asked that the small animal be examined and boarded but added that she couldn't stay.

"Late for work, huh? No problem. We'll examine her and call for your consent if we need to treat—"

"No, I'll be out, you know, fighting fires, and I may not hear my phone. Just do whatever it takes to make her okay and keep her here until I come for her." As the cat had started howling, this whole conversation had a surreal quality that remained as the receptionist agreed to Sophie's requests and disappeared down the hall with the yowling tabby.

"You're going to have to stop allowing everyone to believe you're Sabrina," Jack cautioned her as they drove to the police station. "When the cops start questioning people they'll all report they saw her today. We need everyone to understand that she's missing."

"I didn't think of it that way," Sophie said. "Okay, I'm now Sophie Sparrow again, unlikely look-alike."

He smiled at her.

At the police station, they spoke to a Detective Reece, a very tall man with a thick thatch of gray hair and a sweet smile that seemed as if it would be better suited for work in the clergy than on the streets. Sophie reported what had transpired outside Sabrina and

Buzz's house. "The guy wore a ski mask and gloves. He pointed a gun at me and I threw the poor cat at him. He fired and I ran. He crashed into a dumpster thing and made a huge mess."

"After that, he proceeded to hit a very solid post," Jack said. "I saw the glitter of glass or plastic in the street. He also fired a shot, as Sophie said. The bullet's undoubtedly there somewhere."

"He probably broke a headlight," Detective Reece said. "I'll get someone out there right away to fetch the pieces and find the bullet. License plate?"

"Obscured," Jack said, "both front and back."

"Anything else?"

Sophie took a deep breath. "I think the cat is going to be okay."

Jack smiled to himself as the detective's eyebrows rose on his forehead.

In the end, there was no way to know if it was the same man who had tried to run Sophie over in the hotel garage or if he was responsible for the origami, let alone Sabrina's absence. They were told the lab work on the food samples hadn't come back yet, that there were no prints on the origami fox found on the breakfast tray and that Sabrina's car was still missing. But Detective Reece, as opposed to Sergeant Jones down in Seaport, seemed to take the situation more seriously and Sophie felt as though he would actually see things through.

They left after answering a host of related questions and drove immediately to the fire station, where they were told they could find Sue Landers in the kitchen but that Kyle Woods was off for a few days.

The kitchen was large and well equipped, and at the center of it, a woman stood peering into an open refrigerator. A pile of ingredients sat on the counter next to her. At the sound of her name, she straightened up and turned. They were treated to a blazing-white smile and curious hazel eyes surrounded by an unruly mass of red hair and a galaxy of freckles. She stared openmouthed at Sophie before saying, "Sabrina never told me she had a twin."

"That's kind of up in the air," Sophie said evasively.

"You could have fooled me. Just your hair and the mole on your cheek are different. You aren't Sabrina playing a trick on me, are you?"

"No, definitely not."

"The resemblance is amazing."

Jack got her back on track by showing her the picture of the guy in the hooded sweatshirt and she shook her head as she closed the fridge. "He doesn't look familiar," she said.

"So you never saw him hanging around the station waiting for Sabrina?"

"Are you saying this is *another* friend of hers?"

"Another?" Jack asked.

She shook her head as she opened a cupboard and rifled through the contents. "Never mind. This dude's a friend, though?"

"No," Jack said. "Listen, I'll level with you. The police will be around asking questions sooner or later because Sabrina seems to have disappeared." He explained about being Buzz's friend and that Sabrina had called him to help her but vanished before he could do more than take a few random photos.

"It's hard to tell with Sabrina," Sue said carefully as she closed the cupboard. "She can run hot and cold. I don't mean that in a bad way. She's just, well, independent. If she was having a problem of some sort she'd probably tell Kyle about it before she'd tell me."

"Kyle Woods?" Jack said.

"Yeah. But he's up in Canada visiting his grandfather for a few days."

"So, Sabrina, you and Kyle are close friends?"

"Sort of," she said. "Kyle is married but his wife walked out on him right before the holidays. Since then, he and Sabrina have been hanging out. Well, you know, he's suddenly alone and so is she thanks to Buzz's job." She peered at Sophie again. "You say Sabrina is missing?"

"Yes. She asked Jack for help and then she left the hotel in her car and no one has seen or heard from her since."

"I wouldn't worry," Sue said casually.

"Why not?" Jack asked.

"She may have gotten a wild hair and just taken off. Or she may have met someone she knew. You said the police are looking for her?"

"They will be. I'm sure they'll ask you questions."

Sue shook her head as she glanced back at the fridge. "She has this whole week off. I'm not going to start worrying about her until she doesn't show up for her next shift. Listen, it's my turn to cook and that means enchiladas. I can't find the tortillas. If Rowdy forgot to buy them, I'm going to have to kill him. You guys need anything else?"

"Is there anyone else here who she might have confided in?"

Sue seemed to consider the question before responding. "I don't think so. Kyle will be back by the end of the week. Chances are if she had plans, she told him." She patted her pocket and took out a card. "Feel free to call me if you think I can help. But like I said, Sabrina is a take-no-prisoners type of gal. Try not to worry too much."

They talked to the supervisor and anyone else they could corner, but no one recognized the guy in the photo and no one had heard from Sabrina or expected to.

"Did you get the feeling Sue thinks something is going on between Kyle Woods and Sabrina?" Sophie asked after they got back in his car.

"Yeah, I did. Well, he's off for a few days, she's off—I don't know. I don't want to think it, but you have to keep an open mind. What she does is her business— and Buzz's. I just want her safe."

"Would you be this easygoing if you suspected your spouse was fooling around?" she asked him as she put on her seat belt.

He turned his head to smile at her as he started the engine. "Hell no."

Sophie stared back at the station house with a million random thoughts flying through her head. Jack let the car idle as he touched her arm. "What is it?" he asked. "What's on your mind?"

"I was just thinking about Sabrina. About her house and her job and her habits… She's a brave woman, isn't she?"

"Well, yes, I suppose she is."

"But she's also a good friend to people. Sue made her sound a little cold and calculating but that's not the woman I saw in her emails. People obviously relied on her in different ways. She drove for Meals on Wheels, she visited a friend's grandmother in a dementia care facility, she helped a friend called Bunny when her marriage broke up… She's a kind person."

He smiled. "It sounds as if you're comparing yourself to her."

"We're nothing alike," Sophie said.

"Other than your appearances, there's the fact that you both love or loved a man named Daniel."

"Love? Maybe she does, but my Danny was never a lover."

"Then what was he, Sophie? What *is* he?"

She met his gaze. "I'm not sure."

He took a deep breath but went back to his original point. "You both have tabby cats, you both vacation at the same seaside town and even stay at the same hotel, albeit at different times of the year."

"Coincidences," Sophie said.

"Perhaps. But you're also both kind and civic minded, and don't shake your head at me. I bet you do a lot more for the kids you teach than show up in the classroom, don't you?"

"Yeah. You know. But I get back so much more than I give."

"That sounds like the essence of compassion to me," he said. "Besides, you're both very beautiful on the outside, too."

She laughed to cover a sudden onslaught of shyness. "I never felt beautiful before meeting you," she said and looked away at once, wishing she could take back her words. They were true, but they also revealed the very vulnerable core at the center of her being.

"I'm not a fool," she added at once so he wouldn't have to figure out how to respond to the neediness of her last comment. "Sabrina and I look too much alike for it to be a fluke. All my life I've been searching for someone—I thought it was a forever guy, you know, true love and all that. But now I think I was searching for Sabrina. And since I can't compare notes with her, I have to talk to my mother, I have to know exactly what she's been keeping from me and why."

"When are you going to talk to her?"

"Tonight. It's time for me to go home and face my family."

"Including Danny?"

"Yes. I have a huge diamond to return."

"I'm going with you," Jack said, and for some reason she wasn't surprised.

"Okay."

"No argument?"

"Until they catch the idiot in the white car, you are more than welcome to watch my back. I guess I have to ask if going to Portland isn't a waste of your time. Your priority is Sabrina."

"My priority is getting her back in her house in time to welcome Buzz home with a giant kiss. You're like a magnet for this white-car guy and at this point he's my sole lead."

"Okay, but I need to go back and get my car. I have a job to return to on Tuesday."

"It'll be harder to throw the guy in the car off the trail if we're driving two cars," he warned her. "He's got to be somewhere close. He always is."

She shuddered as a dozen spidery chills radiated outward from her spinal column. "I have to admit all this is getting to me. I'm normally a fly-under-the-radar type of gal, not the kind anyone tries to kill."

"I don't think anyone wants to actually kill *you*, as in the Sophia Sparrow you," Jack said.

"That's the only me I am. And how do we know what this lunatic is thinking? Maybe he's declared war on all dark-haired girls who own tabby cats."

He laughed softly in his throat.

"I'll just say it," she added, her voice deadly serious. "Sabrina may be courageous, but I'm not Sabrina. I'm a card-carrying chicken."

"Once again you sell yourself short," Jack said. "Okay, we'll go get your car. I'm going to twist and turn all over this city to try to throw him off, so try to keep up."

"Just watch me," she said and took a deep breath.

"That's exactly what I intend to do," he responded.

Chapter Six

By the time they reached the outskirts of Portland, Jack was hungry enough to eat just about anything, including fast food. He passed Sophie's car and signaled as he pulled into a restaurant parking lot, relieved when she followed suit.

They went inside and ordered, then sat at a window table and unwrapped burgers and fries. It was useless trying to maintain a conversation with Sophie; the closer she got to home, the more preoccupied she became. At one point she dug in her purse and brought out an enormous diamond ring that she turned this way and that as she studied it. He had no idea what she was thinking. He began to wonder if it was such a good idea to go with her into what promised to be a powder keg, but when he suggested she drop him off at a hotel and continue on without him, she shook her head.

"Oh, no you don't," she said, stuffing the ring in her pants pocket. "I'm not going in there alone. Besides, what about the phony Gerald Duff?"

"Good point. Okay, I'll stay outside. That way you'll have your privacy and I can keep an eye on the street."

"Cluck, cluck, cluck. Jack, don't wimp out on me," she scolded.

"I just don't want to make things harder for you."

She stuffed her uneaten food in the bag. "I'm finished. Let's go."

He looked longingly at the half of burger he was about to abandon and grabbed a handful of fries as they left.

Sophie's childhood home turned out to be a modest dwelling on a quiet street. Even in the dark with light rain falling, he could see the place reflected its owner's warmth. The shutters were painted bright yellow, the house itself a dove gray, and tubs that probably spent the spring and summer spilling over with flowers sat on either side of the front door.

She parked right in front and immediately got out. He did the same, habitually scanning the road for any sign of a white sedan—now with a broken headlight and dented bumper—before following her up a cement path.

The front door of the house opened while they were still a few feet away. A tall woman stood glowering at them. "I expected you hours ago," she said. "Hurry, there's just time for you to freshen up."

As they walked into the light from the porch fixture, the woman—she had to be Sophie's formidable mother—clutched her throat. "What happened to your hair?" she gasped.

"I dyed it," Sophie said.

"Go wash it."

"Why?" Sophie asked as they both paused on the

small porch. The mother still barricaded the door and so far she hadn't paid Jack the least bit of attention.

"Because it looks stupid. Danny will—"

"Danny? You called him? He's coming here? Now?"

"He'll be here any minute. Now go wash that stuff out of your hair." She finally met Jack's gaze and added, "Who are you?"

"This is my friend Jack Travers," Sophie said. "Jack, my mother, Margaret Sparrow. Mom, it's wet and cold out here. How about you let us in?"

"'Us'?" she repeated, but stepped aside for them to enter. The room Jack found himself in was small, overly warm and dominated by a reclining chair and a television set.

Margaret Sparrow slid Jack a sidelong look. "What is he doing here?" she asked Sophie.

"Like I said, he's a friend. Mom, I need to talk to you about something serious."

"First fetch me a glass of water," Margaret said. "All this stress has taken its toll. Honestly, Sophie, you've been very inconsiderate to everyone."

"I'll get the water," Jack volunteered. Sophie gestured toward an arch to his left.

Margaret's voice followed Jack into the small kitchen.

"The only thing you need to worry about right now," she said, "is making sure you don't blow it again with Danny. Get rid of this other man."

"Mother…"

"Help me sit down. My sciatica is worse than ever."

Jack returned with the water right as Sophie assisted

her mother into the recliner. He handed the glass to Sophie, as Margaret was busy sorting through a dozen prescription bottles until she found the one she wanted.

Once the medicine was taken, Sophie tried again. "I need to ask you about a woman named Sabrina Long Cromwell."

"Never heard of her," Margaret said. She glanced at the wall clock and added, "There's no time to fix your hair, although, Lordy, what were you thinking? And where'd you get that sweater? It hides your figure. Go change."

"Mom," Sophie said again. "Forget Danny. Did you know there's a woman who lives two hours away from here who looks exactly like me? How is that possible?"

"How should I know? Stop going on about nothing and show this guy the door. Your fiancé will be here any moment. Isn't that a lot more important than some girl you don't know?"

Jack thought he detected a little tic in Margaret's left eye that suggested she wasn't as nonplussed about the mention of a Sophie look-alike as she tried to appear.

There was no way he was wading into this fray, however. He strove to make his six-foot-plus frame a little less obtrusive by standing far to the side, but it was a small room in a house with low ceilings.

Sophie stood her ground. "No, Danny is not more important than getting to the bottom of this. Jack, will you please show my mother Sabrina's wedding picture?"

He pulled out his phone and found the photo. Walking to Margaret's side, he turned the phone so she could see. He was standing close enough that he felt her body stiffen as Sabrina's face filled the small screen.

"Remarkable, isn't it?" Sophie asked as she took Jack's phone from his hand and looked at the picture again as if to reacquaint herself.

"There is a surface resemblance," her mother allowed.

"Will you please tell me how this could happen?"

Margaret shook her head. "I don't have the slightest idea." To Jack, her voice sounded sincere, as though she truly was flummoxed.

Sophie perched on the edge of the small sofa next to her mother's recliner. "Mom, just tell me. Am I adopted?"

"Are you adopted? Stop being silly."

"Then how—"

"I don't know!" Margaret snapped.

Sophie laid her free hand atop her mom's arm. "I have a theory," she said softly.

This was news to Jack, who tried once again to disappear into the woodwork.

"Honestly, this isn't the time—" Margaret began, but Sophie cut through her protest.

"If I am truly not adopted, then I think Dad talked you into having a baby. When you found out you were going to have twins, I think the idea of raising two kids when you didn't even really want one was too much for you to handle. I think you gave my sister up for adoption. I don't know how you talked Dad into that. Maybe he didn't even know, maybe you kept it a secret—"

"Listen to yourself," her mother interrupted. "Do you realize how delusional you sound?"

"Then you tell me what happened," Sophie said. "Please, Mom. I need to know. I can't pretend to understand how you might have felt—I've never been in a similar position—but surely you can see that I must know the truth."

Sophie might not think she was as brave as Sabrina, Jack thought, but broaching this subject in the middle of the Danny debacle wasn't exactly an easy thing to do, not when deep inside her world pivoted on this key piece of missing information.

"You want the truth?" Margaret said. "Well, here it is. I had one baby. You. Not two." She stared hard at Sophie as if daring defiance.

"You can't sweep this under the rug," Sophie said. "It's important, damn it."

"How dare you swear at me!"

"And how dare you lie to me," Sophie said. "I'm not leaving here until you tell the truth."

"You want the truth? Come with me."

With that, the older woman waved away Sophie's help and struggled to her feet. "I'll show you the truth," she muttered, and grabbed a cane. The two women exited the room through another doorway while Jack stood there wondering what he should do.

A soft knock on the door answered that question. He opened it to find a clean-shaven man about his own age. "What can I do for you?" Jack asked the sandy-haired thirtysomething guy, who wore a very expensive Burberry coat. It had to be Danny, and face it, Jack was curious what Sophie had seen in him.

"I'm looking for my fiancée, Sophia Sparrow," he said. "My name is Daniel Privet."

"Come on in." Jack scanned the street for white cars before he closed the door.

The newcomer looked around the empty room. "Where is she?"

Jack waved toward the back of the house. "She and her mother are…visiting." He stared at the guy in the better light. Something about him seemed familiar.

"What are you staring at?" Danny asked, his brows furled.

"Sorry. I was just wondering if we've met."

"I don't recall it if we did."

"You just look kind of familiar."

"I work up in Seattle at a law firm called Finder and Finch," Danny said. "Well, I should say I used to work there. I've recently taken a position here in Portland with another firm. Sophie and I are getting married soon."

"That's not what I heard," Jack said, curious how Danny would react to direct confrontation.

"What's that supposed to mean?"

"Sophie never agreed to marry you."

"She most certainly did. Right here in this room, as a matter of fact. Who in the hell are you?"

"Jack Travers. I'm a friend of Sophie's. I'm curious about something. Why in the world did you propose in front of her mom?"

"I don't see how that's any of your business," Danny said as a red flush began to creep up his neck.

"Was it because you needed her on your side? That's all I can figure. You were unsure what Sophie would say so you used her mother to, well, gang up on her. That's it, right?"

His cheeks were bright pink by now. "I'm quite intimate with this family," he said sternly. "Sophie's never mentioned your name."

"We just met a day or so ago," Jack said as he heard Sophie and her mother returning to the living room.

"Now are you satisfied?" Margaret asked as she headed for her chair.

"No," Sophie said from right behind her.

Danny rushed forward and threw his arms around Sophie. "Darling," he gushed. "You're back!" He caressed her hair, apparently oblivious to the way she tried to push herself free. "If you only knew how worried I've been about you."

Sophie firmly detached herself from his grip. "Danny—"

"Shush, sweetie, I have the most wonderful news! I changed our flight to Hawaii. We leave tomorrow! We can get married out there and have two whole weeks to get used to being Mr. and Mrs. Daniel Privet. I'm sure your mother will understand."

"Of course I do," Margaret chirped from the recliner.

Jack watched all of this as one might view a reality television show. It was downright surreal how the two attempted to cut Sophie out of her own life.

"We're not getting married in Hawaii or anywhere else," she said softly.

Margaret's deep sigh sucked half the air out of the room. "I don't know what's gotten into you," she lamented. Then she looked straight at Jack. "It has to be you. You put some kind of spell on her."

"Do you really think she's that gullible?" Jack asked.

Sophie reached into her jeans pocket and emerged with the diamond ring she'd stuffed there when they ate dinner. She held her hand toward Danny. "I'm sorry, I really am," she said. "You must take this back. I have no intention of marrying anyone. I think it's best if we stop seeing each other."

"You don't mean that," Danny said, refusing to take back the ring.

"Yes, I do mean it."

He shook his head. "I know you love me. We're going to get married just like I…we…planned. I'll make you happy, I swear I will."

For the first time, he seemed to notice the phone Sophie still clutched in her left hand.

"What's that!" he demanded, turning his head to better see Sabrina's picture. He grabbed the phone away and stared openmouthed at her image. "You got married!" he screeched, and then turned to Jack. "Is this you in the picture? Did you two… How could you?" he demanded of Sophie. "After all the time I've invested."

"'Time you've invested'?"

He shook his head.

She narrowed her eyes as she forced the ring into his hand. "This isn't a photo of me."

"How is that possible?"

"I don't know how it's possible. We could be twins we look so much alike."

Danny took a step back.

"Do you know her?" Sophie asked. "Her name is Sabrina Cromwell."

He shook his head but the gesture looked as phony as just about every word that had come out of his mouth except for the line about investing time. To Jack that had been the one real thing the man had uttered.

And Jack was positive Danny knew something about Sabrina. On a hunch, he reclaimed his phone and scrolled through the photos, pausing on the one of the guy in the sweatshirt jacket. He showed it to Danny, who retreated another step. "How about this guy. Do you recognize him?"

"No. I've… No."

"I don't know why I didn't see it before," Sophie said wonderingly, looking between the photo and Danny. "This guy bears a surface resemblance to you."

"No way," Danny said, but a light went off in Jack's head. That was the reason he'd thought he'd recognized Danny when he came through the door.

"I used to be a cop," Jack said slowly. "I'm a PI now. In today's world that means I know my way around a computer. Give me an hour and I can trace your whole family tree back to the gleam in your great-great-grandpa's eyes. You can save me the hour and make it easy on yourself by telling us what you know.

Oh, and maybe it will jar your memory if I tell you he tried to kill Sophie."

"Twice," Sophie added.

Danny stared at her. "He tried to hurt you?"

"He tried to *kill* me."

"Why would he do that?"

"Apparently because he thinks I'm Sabrina. By the way, she's missing. The police are looking for this guy in connection to her disappearance and the attacks on me. If you know something you'd better speak up."

Danny reminded Jack of a groundhog who peeks out of his hole and doesn't like what he sees.

"Mr. Privet, face it," Jack said. "You're stuck between a rock and a hard place. Keep in mind we're going to tell the investigating police our suspicion that you have information. To stay silent now makes you an accessory after the fact…"

"He's my half brother," Danny blurted out, "but you're wrong, he couldn't have had anything to do with hurting someone or trying to kill Sophie. That's insane."

"What's his name?"

"I don't know."

"You don't know your brother's name?"

"We were never close, never. He ended up in prison a few years ago. I heard he's out now and I heard he changed his name, you know, for a fresh start. I don't know what he chose because I don't have anything to do with him."

"I thought you just said he'd never hurt anyone,"

Sophie said. "How do you know that if you're alienated from him?"

Danny bit at his lip and shook his head.

"What about your mother?" she asked. "You said she works for a guy up in Seattle. I can't remember who the guy is, but she'll know your half brother's new name."

"She quit that job. She's…traveling."

"But you can get in touch with her."

It took him a moment to respond. "I doubt it," he finally said.

"How about your half brother's old name?" Jack asked.

"The guy's a loose cannon," Danny grumbled without making eye contact with anyone.

"If your half brother has been in prison I can find his name in about five seconds."

"Then find it," Danny said.

Anger chilled Jack's voice as he looked Danny in the eye. "Whether you like it or not, you're in this up to your eyeballs. Do you know where Sabrina is? So help me if anything happens to her or to Sophie, I'll wring your neck with my bare hands."

Danny collapsed on the small sofa as though his feet would no longer support his weight. "Oh, God," he groaned, covering his head with his hands.

"Stop badgering the poor boy," Margaret Sparrow ordered. Was she really so blinded by Danny's show of wealth that she couldn't see what a complete waste of skin and bones he was? Jack fought an urgent desire to whisk Sophie away. How she had managed to mature into womanhood with even an ounce of self-esteem was a miracle to him.

But the bigger fish that needed frying sat crumpled on the sofa. He obviously knew more than he'd told them so far and even their warnings about the police didn't seem to get to him.

"Tell us his name, new, old, whatever," Jack insisted. "Is it Privet like yours?"

"We're so worried about Sabrina," Sophie added. "If your half brother can help find her—"

Danny slammed his fist against his thigh and shot to his feet. "I don't have to talk to you two," he said, glancing from Sophie to Jack. He stabbed a finger at Sophie. "You blew it, babe." He strode to the door with an attempt at a swagger.

"Danny, wait, where are you going?" Margaret pleaded.

He opened the door and looked back at them all. "If I have to talk to the police, I'll talk to the police, but I'd rather live out my life on a deserted island than spend one more second in this terrible house. You can all go to hell." And at that, he left without closing the door.

Jack glanced over at Sophie, who looked introspective as she watched Danny's retreat. He bet she was wondering what she'd ever seen in the slimeball.

"I'm going to go make a call," Jack announced as he swung the door shut and walked into the kitchen for a little privacy.

By the time he gave the Astoria police Danny's name so they could start tracing his relatives and got caught up on what was happening at their end, he was ready to leave. He returned to the living room to find both women more or less as he had left them. He was desperate to drive to Seattle. He wasn't sure if Sophie would come with him or elect to stay here and try to fix her small family.

"I want you out of my house," Margaret said as she glared at Jack.

"If he goes, I go," Sophie said.

"Did I raise an idiot? We need to put our heads together and figure out a way to fix what's happened with Danny. He'll give you everything you want if you play your cards right."

Sophie looked at her mother as though she'd never seen her before. "You mean he'll give me everything *you* want."

"It's the same thing," Margaret said.

"No, Mom, it isn't. And besides, that ship has sailed—for both of us." She glanced down at the floor as she took a deep breath, then she leaned over and retrieved the diamond ring that must have rolled under the sofa when Danny stood so abruptly. She set it on her mother's tray. "Maybe you can hock this," she said. She picked up her purse from the chair where she'd flung it and without another word, opened the front door and exited the house.

"She can't just leave," Margaret said.

Jack stared at her a moment. "You're lucky she

stayed as long as she did," he said, and left to join Sophie before a white car could appear out of nowhere and run her down.

Chapter Seven

The rain had stopped and the skies cleared to the point where a few stars actually glimmered in the sky. But the temperature had dropped and Sophie's coat wasn't really warm enough. Still, she ignored her own car and leaned against Jack's. In retrospect, she wished she'd packed a bag before her big exit, as she was still wearing the clothes she'd dressed in Saturday morning and it was now ten o'clock Sunday night. No way was she going back inside.

"You're going with me?" Jack asked as he approached.

She smiled as she watched his easy gait. The past hour or so had been an exercise in humiliating chaos that was going to take a while to process. But there had been a constant: Jack. He alone stood out as a person without a selfish agenda. He'd defended her without acting like she couldn't take care of herself, treated her like the intelligent, thoughtful human being she was beginning to hope she would become.

That was not to say she'd banished all her insecurities, self-doubts or the persistent desire to hide under a rock, just that she also saw glimmers of confidence and self-worth. Somehow they made her feel stronger, more substantial, and she had Jack, in part, to thank. And, perversely, she also owed Danny. He'd held a mirror up to her face; seeing herself through his eyes was sobering.

But that led to a giant question: What had been the purpose of his "investment" in her? It didn't make any sense.

"Sophie?" Jack asked and she shook her head.

"Sorry, my thoughts wandered."

"I don't doubt it." He looked back at the house and raised his hand. "That whole, uh—"

"Freak show?"

He smiled. "Yeah. It was something else. Frankly, your mother and Danny are made for each other."

"I know. So, how about it, are you driving to Seattle to try to find Danny's mother?"

"It would make more sense to use the internet but if she's as slippery as her son, a phone call would accomplish squat."

"Plus Danny said she was traveling, whatever that means."

"Do you believe him?"

"I don't know what to believe. I need to talk to her, too. It would save gas if we rode together."

"I guess it would," he said as though he might not want the company. She knew he did. He looked up and down the street, no doubt for a white car, before unlocking the doors. The two of them sat in silence for a moment until Jack said, "I guess the only trouble is where do we start?"

"Aha," she said. She'd been waiting for him to ask. "Thanks to Danny's big mouth, I was able to connect the dots. Remember how he said his half brother was a loose cannon? And then he said that whole thing about how he'd rather be stuck on a deserted island than in my house."

"Okay," Jack said. "I'm listening."

"A week or two ago I saw a letter in his car. The return address label said it was from someone named R. H. Cannon, Weather Island, Washington. Someone had crossed out the R. H. Cannon part and handwritten the initials N.R. above the label. I asked Danny about it and he blew me off. At the time, I thought N.R. might be the name of an old girlfriend but then I remembered his mom's name is Nora. I'm not sure her last name begins with an R, but I'll bet you a dollar that letter was from his mother and that R. H. Cannon is the name of the man she works for. Danny told me the guy lived in Seattle. Well, Weather Island is just a forty-minute ferry ride away."

"I've never heard of Weather Island," Jack said.

Sophie smothered a yawn. "I went there with my dad when I was a kid."

He started the car. "Let's give it a try. But listen, Seattle is only about three or four hours away. Let's get a room for the night on the outskirts of town and drive the distance tomorrow morning."

"We'd have to get an early start if we want to catch the first ferry."

"Then we'll get an early start. It's been a very long day."

"Okay," she said. "Only I'll have to borrow your pajama top again."

"No problem. You look a hell of a lot sexier in it than I do."

She doubted that. "As long as we get up there before Danny has a chance to blow the whistle. I want to be back here by tomorrow night. Maybe by then Sabrina will be home and this whole thing will be over."

"I hope so," he said, but she detected no real confidence in his voice.

"Now you've got me hoping she's having an affair with fireman Kyle. At least that would mean she's safe."

"I got an email from Buzz saying he's coming home. It'll take him a couple of days…but he's on his way."

"Did he sound worried?"

"He didn't say it outright—everyone who knows Sabrina respects that independent streak in her—but if he's cutting the study short, that's a pretty good indicator he's concerned."

To Sophie, the reality of Sabrina's absence seemed to come and go. For hours now she'd clung to Sue's assurances that Sabrina would show up when she wanted to, but now, sitting here in the dark and thinking back over a day that had started with an origami fox on their breakfast tray and still wasn't over, it didn't seem quite so likely. "I should have asked Danny if his half brother knows how to make origami."

"That would have been smart," Jack said as he turned the key. "However, there was quite a bit going on."

"No kidding. Did the Astoria police have information about anything?"

"They told me to call back tomorrow, which is understandable. Detective Reece went home hours ago, so I left a message with all the information. When I call him in the morning, I'll give him Danny's name and his half brother's information again. He'll be able to get a last name for us in case his mother has flown the coop. I'll also give him Kyle Woods's name and ask him to make sure Kyle wasn't using the old guy as a ruse to get away for a private meeting with Sabrina. I just want to know she's safe and bring her home."

"Home," Sophie said, reeling at the mention of the word. Up until an hour ago, she'd had one, but now—no, now she didn't. "I don't have a home anymore," she said aloud to come to terms with it.

"Technically, that house is still yours, not your mother's."

"Do you really believe that?" she asked him as she leaned back against the headrest.

"Not if you don't," he said. He reached over to grip her arm in support. She caught his fingers and he glanced at her.

"Thank you," she said. "For going in there with me. For…everything."

She liked that he didn't pretend not to understand what she meant. He squeezed her hand in his and then released it. "You're welcome."

They found a hotel easily and without even asking, Jack rented a single room with two beds. Sophie washed out her underwear, put on Jack's pajama top and crawled into bed. She watched his face as he worked on his laptop. He sure was easy to look at but it went deeper than the surface with him. She enjoyed the mobility of his expressions, the untold stories in his eyes.

Up until now, she'd acknowledged to herself that she really liked him. Liked spending time with him, liked talking to him. She felt his protective vibe without being overwhelmed by it, and for the first time since losing her dad, it seemed someone thought her idiosyncrasies endearing rather than stupid.

But there was a wall between them, too, and it wasn't just Sabrina's disappearance or the incident in the street outside Sabrina's house. It was also Danny's belligerence and her own mother's selfish greed. She'd been on a roller coaster the last two days—so much had happened that was making her rethink her entire life.

"The good news is Daniel Privet really was an attorney with Finder and Finch," Jack said. "He's not listed anymore, though, so I guess they took him off their list real fast. I also checked the ferry schedules. It's a private company that services some of the smaller islands, including Weather Island, and it leaves Seattle at seven forty-five." He closed his laptop and got to his feet. "And you're right, a guy named Randall Harrison Cannon lives there. I couldn't get a name on a housekeeper. Not knowing her last name is problematic. I could run further searches on Danny to get to his mom but since we're going there anyway, I'll save that for later. I'm bushed," he added as he set the alarm on his phone.

A few minutes later he came out of the bathroom wearing his pajama bottoms. No T-shirt tonight. A light coating of fine dark hair highlighted his pectoral muscles and his taut torso. Last night she'd found his nudeness an annoying distraction. Tonight she found it absolutely captivating.

He sat down on the edge of his bed, put his phone on the nightstand and looked at her. She waited for him to say something but he didn't. The fact that his gaze didn't make her squirm kind of stunned her.

"What are you thinking?" she asked at last.

"I'm thinking you're an amazing woman," he said.

She smiled. "Do you think so?"

"You've conquered a lot of negativity and you've done it with your sanity intact. I admire that."

"Thank you," she whispered.

"How did you do it?" he asked.

"I had a wonderful father. To this day I don't know how he and Mother ever got together. He was nurturing and kind and sweet tempered, but just like me, he was never enough for her. He sold shoes for a living, the same job for twenty years. He was so proud when someone specifically sought his help…but he didn't make a lot of money and Mom was always pressuring him to make something out of himself."

"She couldn't see that he already had," Jack said.

She nodded. "He was happy."

"And he adored you."

She nodded as tears flooded her eyes.

Jack got down on his knees beside her. He swept hair from her forehead and kissed the exposed skin. "I think he lives inside of you," Jack said. "Is there any better gift to give a beloved child?"

"What if I'm not his child?"

"You mean, what if you're adopted?"

"Yes."

"So what?" Jack said. "He was your dad, and like it or not, Margaret is your mother. They raised you, they loved you, well, each in their own way."

"I know," she said. "I'm sorry about the tears."

He plucked a tissue from the box on the nightstand and handed it to her as she sat up. The warmth of his blue eyes was a hypnotic embrace that drew her to him. "Danny was using me," she said as she dabbed the moistness from her eyes.

"I know."

"Why?"

"You're beautiful and sexy. No man could resist you."

"Jack, you know that's not true. He didn't find me alluring at all. I was an investment to him. But in what way? It doesn't make sense."

"We're going to find out," he said. "It's too big a coincidence that his half brother has apparently been stalking Sabrina and now is going after you. Hopefully the police will wring the truth out of Danny and we can get this thing wrapped up."

His focus had dropped to her mouth as he spoke. She could read his mounting desire as clearly as if it was written on his face. Was that because she shared it?

His face drifted toward hers and their lips touched. They separated immediately. Sophie smiled. He kissed her again as they fell back together on her bed.

She had never been kissed with such abandon, with

such intensity or purpose. His fingers stroked the soft flesh of her throat, down to the hollow at the base, under the pajama top to brush along her clavicles... His lips followed their path and for a moment she was lost in the sheer ecstasy of unexpected and glorious sensations.

"Jack," she heard herself say. Her voice sounded as though it came from a distant knoll.

Time seemed to stop for a moment or two, then they both started speaking at the same time. "You first," he said.

With a mental kick to her stupid psyche, she whispered the truth. "No matter how good this feels on the outside, on the inside I'm just not ready. I can't go from Danny to you in one day. It's not who I am."

"I hate that guy," he whispered.

"This isn't about him."

"I know that." He propped himself up on his elbow, gazed into her eyes and gently brushed her face with his fingers as though unable to keep from touching her. As her own hand currently ran along his biceps, she understood the compulsion completely.

"The first time we met I thought you were someone else," he said in a soft sexy voice that reverberated inside Sophie. "What was really confusing was that to me, at that time, you were my best friend's wife who I'd always thought pretty but distant. And then suddenly you'd grown warm and desirable. It really shook me. I can't tell you what a relief it was when you turned out to be...well, you."

Her smile deepened. "You felt something that soon?"

"Yeah. Now don't laugh, but I'd had the premonition, if you want to call it that, that answering Sabrina's call was kind of like responding to the call of destiny. When I met you—well, I knew I'd been right. It felt as though everything in my life had been leading to that moment. We were meant to meet each other. There's a bigger plan for us. Does that sound whacky?"

"Yeah, it does," she said. "But I kind of get it. The flip side of that is I never dreamed you'd look twice at a woman like me."

"And I can't take my eyes off you," he said, smiling. He leaned forward and kissed her lips, then gently grasped her chin and looked into her eyes. "When the time is right, I want you. All of you. Tell me when the moment arrives that you feel the same way about me and I don't care where we are or what we're doing, I'm going to take your body to places it's never been."

"That's quite a promise," she said.

He smiled and kissed her nose. "I'm good for my word."

"I'll make sure to buy some sexy lingerie," she added as he slipped out of her arms and stood up.

He stared down at her. "You won't need any lingerie."

She watched him get in the other bed, and once again their gazes met. She was already second-guessing her judgment.

"Good night, Sophia Sparrow," he said softly as he turned off the light.

"Good night," she whispered and closed her eyes.

Instead of sleep, she found herself reentering what

would always be Margaret Sparrow's house no matter who held the mortgage papers. Her mother's refusal to acknowledge Sophie's very real concerns about discovering a look-alike still rankled her. As proof that Sophie was being ridiculous, she'd produced a picture of herself sitting atop a bed holding a newborn in a pink blanket. "See?" she'd said. "One baby. Not two."

"This proves nothing," Sophie had responded.

"It proves everything. If you still don't believe me, look at this."

She'd turned the page to reveal a picture of her father holding her in his arms. He was standing in the kitchen, warming a baby bottle in a pan on the stove. He held a six-month-old Sophie against his chest and his smile jumped from the page.

There was a single high chair to his left. Not two. One.

Your father would never have given away a baby. That was the unspoken message between Sophie and her mother. *You don't trust me, I get it, but you do trust him, don't you?*

And the answer was yes, she did trust her father, his big heart, his homespun wisdom, his love. He'd been her rock and she'd missed him every day since an untimely heart attack stole him away.

But that trust didn't obliterate the fact that as far as Sophie could tell, Sabrina and she were identical except for a mole on Sophie's cheek. If her parents didn't have two babies of their own, then they adopted her. Why keep that a secret?

Maybe it was Sabrina's mother who had been unable to care for two. Maybe she'd shared her windfall of babies and exacted a promise of silence. "Back in the day, did you know a woman with the last name of Long?" Sophie had whispered.

Her mother hadn't flinched. "Long? No. Why?"

"I need Sabrina," Sophie mumbled.

Jack's voice responded although she couldn't understand what he was saying. Her eyes flicked open and she realized she'd been dreaming and that she hadn't spoken aloud.

"Lisa," he moaned in the same forsaken voice as the night before.

His cry was what had awoken her.

And right that second, Sophie realized why she'd really turned Jack away. She wasn't the only one with bridges to burn and demons to excise.

She got out of bed. This time when her weight hit the mattress he reached for her. No tight grasp, just open arms. She slid beneath the covers to lie beside him, her goal to comfort, but his goal was different. His hot mouth claimed hers, his hands moved down her body, grasping her rear, pulling her so close even the layers of cloth between them seemed to burn away. She felt his hand reach under the pajama top, travel up her thigh, across her belly, cup her breast. He pulled her closer and she was enveloped by a man bigger, hotter and sexier than any she could have ever created in her imagination.

In a moment, he would make love to her.

"Sophie," he whispered into her hair. "Sophie, Sophie." She kissed him hard and long, his voice floating her name like a blanket to warm her heart. He knew exactly who she was, exactly whose body he touched, whose arms encircled him.

His hand sliding between her legs drove all thought from her mind. She pulled at his pajama bottoms as he pushed aside the pajama top.

One hand tangled in her hair, the other touched her breasts tenderly. In a moment he would be inside her. She felt conflicted, half ready and half worried that for him, lovemaking had started with a memory of one woman before distilling into the realization of another. Of her. It was even possible he might still think she was Lisa even though he'd called out Sophie's name.

He'd told her what he wanted from her—absolute commitment to the moment—not doubt and indecision.

The whites of his eyes as he gazed down at her glistened and he grew still as if sensing her sudden detachment. He kissed her lips briefly as he lowered his head next to hers. His weight seemed to double before he rolled onto his back beside her. His fingers entwined with hers.

After a minute, he kissed her forehead and gripped her shoulders. "Lisa, right?"

"You woke with another nightmare."

"Damn."

"Jack?"

"You want to know about her."

"Yes."

He sighed. "I don't even know where to start."

"What was she like?"

"Pretty. Dark hair, blue eyes, smart, funny. She

was studying prelaw because her father wanted her to. What she wanted was to be a famous chef with her own television show. She worked at this little bistro to try to get experience. Someone from a magazine saw her in the kitchen and offered her a spread in a series they were doing called 'Coeds Cook!' She was very excited—this was her big chance. They said they'd send a photographer to take a few informal pictures of her whipping up a marinara sauce to make sure she came across sexy enough."

"Sexy enough? For a cooking magazine?"

"Yeah. That's what I thought. But the magazine turned out to be one of those titillating college girl things. I told her the article would include two sentences about cooking and two pages of photos of her wearing damn near nothing but an apron. She went ballistic, told me I didn't respect her decisions, etcetera. I don't know, maybe she was right, maybe I didn't understand then how important it all was to her. Anyway, I saw her a couple of days later and she said the photo shoot had gone great and she was on her way to see the pictures. She'd completely forgotten we had a longstanding date to go to a concert. I stormed off. That was the last time I ever saw her."

Sophie knew there was more. She could feel his despair in her own bones, pumping through her own veins. She waited.

"She disappeared that night. No one knew where she was. She was just…gone."

"Like Sabrina," Sophie said softly.

"Like Sabrina. I was the major suspect, of course,

until the cops discovered the magazine's photographer had given them an alias and a false address. No one could find out anything about the guy and he was as gone as Lisa was. They made a composite sketch—the guy was tall, dark, walked with a limp. The people who hired him said he didn't talk a lot. One of the typists there said he creeped her out. Long story short, Lisa was found out in the desert a week later. Her body had been set on fire. They had to identify her with dental records. An autopsy determined she'd suffered broken bones before her death… When I think of what she endured before she finally died it breaks my heart."

"And the photographer?"

"They never found him. A composite sketch linked him to another young woman's disappearance although no trace of her body was ever found. After Lisa, apparently, he changed his MO or got run over by a truck, or just flat quit… He just disappeared. No one has ever identified him."

"No wonder Lisa's death haunts you," Sophie said softly, squeezing his fingers with hers.

He turned on his side again, his presence little more than the gleam of his eyes and the musky warm fragrance of his skin. "If I hadn't belittled her big chance, I might have been around during the supposed photo shoot. I might have sensed something about the guy. She might still be alive."

There was no way to respond. He might be right. He might also be wrong but he knew that. She inched closer and he raised his arm so she could nestle against his side.

"I don't have nightmares all the time," he told her softly as he stroked her hair with his free hand. She had thrown one arm across his chest and felt the beat of his heart in her wrist. "It's just that Sabrina said a big man with dark hair had been taking pictures of her while she drained pasta water and then she vanished into thin air. It brought everything back."

"You talked about destiny," Sophie said. "Maybe somehow your past and Sabrina's present are merging."

"That would mean that against all odds she's with a human monster right now. I don't know how to save her from that."

"If it's at all possible, you will," Sophie said, and she glanced at the clock. "We have two hours before we have to leave for Seattle."

"Stay here with me," he whispered.

"Of course," she said simply.

But there was nothing simple about anything.

THEY DROVE TO Seattle under leaden skies, the steely pavement slick with ice as the windshield wipers tried to keep up with the sleet. Sophie was not looking forward to riding a ferry in her thin coat.

Today was a holiday and the schools were closed, but just to be safe, Sophie used the time they spent waiting for the ferry to load to call her principal and arrange for a last-minute substitute-teacher replacement for her class, saying she was indisposed for a week, hoping that was silly, that by tonight they'd have found Sabrina and put this whole thing to rest.

Jack called Detective Reece and found out the detective wasn't in the office.

It was finally their turn to drive aboard and park. The lower deck of the ferry was packed tight with vehicles except for the empty middle lane, as this was a ferry that made four different stops at four different islands. They got out of the car and Sophie studied the other vehicles.

"He couldn't have known we were coming here," Jack said, pulling his coat closer. Sophie knew how he felt. The bottom deck was open on both ends to allow vehicles to move off and on the boat. An icy wind that felt like it carried ice in its gusts blew straight down the middle, whipping loose hair and clothing and torturing warm-blooded creatures. If she wasn't still wearing Jack's blue cashmere sweater, she was certain she would turn into a Popsicle.

"We're the second-to-last stop," Jack added as they climbed the inboard stairs to the second floor.

The heaters were working but the cold still seeped inside. They found an empty bench and sat down. Jack immediately went to work on his phone and Sophie looked through the windows at the sleet-driven skies that merged into the Puget Sound's restless cold water. A small family seated at a nearby table caught her attention and she watched them for a while. The woman looked about her own age. The two children playing checkers beside her were about six or seven, around the age of the kids she taught. For the first time, she seriously wondered what it would be like to have children of her own. With their striking black hair and pretty faces, both the girls could easily be Jack's daughters.

Her daughters.

She smiled at the whimsy and leaned against Jack as fatigue from their interrupted night caught up with her. She actually nodded off, waking only when the ferry pulled against the pier of the first island and more than half the passengers got off, a line of their departing vehicles wending away from the docks as the ferry continued its journey.

"About last night," Jack said as he put away his phone. That got her attention. She was about to tell him that maybe this conversation should wait for another time when he added, "I know it must seem to you that I've never gotten over loving Lisa."

Not what she expected, but as that's exactly how it did seem to her, she nodded.

"My feelings for her are frozen in time," he continued as he took her hand in his, "but I don't harbor fantasies that she and I would have ever lived happily-ever-after. Our profound differences were already driving us apart. That last fight wasn't the first one we'd had, believe me. I've let that part of my past with her go. What remains is the what-if part, my guilt, my failures."

"I can see how that is," Sophie responded. "If Danny had gone slower, if he'd understood the issues between my mother and myself instead of trying to use her to influence me, I might have talked myself into marrying him and if that had happened, it wouldn't have been long before I came to the same realizations that you did."

"The person you choose to love shouldn't be a compromise," he said.

."No, you're right, they shouldn't."

"Love has to come from your heart."

She stared at his lips as he spoke, then glanced to see the mother and her children seated a few feet away. The kids had moved on to a computer game.

"You told me to tell you when I was ready to make love," she whispered.

He laughed softly. "Right here, right now?"

"Well, you assured me I wouldn't need any sexy lingerie, so yep, I'm good to go."

He put an arm around her and kissed her forehead. "In front of those little kids?"

"Oh, I see, you're nothing but a big tease. All talk and no action."

He chuckled as he pulled her head close and kissed her nose. "How about we compromise just this once. You're freezing. There's a sign right over there that promises a snack bar. What'll it be? Hot chocolate or coffee."

"Instead of sex? Better make it the hot chocolate," she said with a big phony sigh. "With marshmallows."

He looked straight into her eyes, opened his mouth and closed it.

"What?" she asked.

"Nothing," he said. "Stay here, I'll be right back."

His phone rang as he stood and he looked at the screen. "Detective Reece," he mouthed to her and, answering the phone in a voice totally at odds with the one he used to speak to her, headed toward the snack bar that was apparently located around the corner amidships.

She leaned her head back against the bulkhead and thought about what he'd said and what he hadn't said. The strange thing was how appalled she'd been by Danny's marriage proposal and vows of undying love after only five weeks. But she'd known Jack for only two days. Two days! The thought of falling in love with him did nothing but cast a rosy glow on her future.

And then a horrible feeling came over her. Danny had used her for some reason she still didn't understand but the truth was she'd used him, too. He'd rescued her, in a way, from herself, given her a diversion. She'd met Jack right smack on the heels of escaping her delusions and latched onto the mystery of Sabrina's absence in order to keep from thinking about her own life. And now she was ready to lose herself in an affair with a man who lived one and a half states away, a man she'd known less than forty-eight hours.

What was wrong with her?

She didn't know what kind of cereal he liked, whom he voted for, if he went to the movies, if he wanted children or liked pancakes or long walks or piña coladas…

She felt the wooden bench vibrate and turned her head as she opened her eyes. "Do you—"

The look on his face stilled her.

He stood up and extended his hand, pulling her to her feet when she took it. "Come on, let's walk," he said.

They took a turn around the interior deck. Sophie could feel Jack's anxiety in his stride and the way his gaze took in every detail of their surroundings, including their fellow passengers. He finally paused before a door leading to the outside deck. "Care to brave the elements?"

"Lead on," she said, shivering at the thought of it.

The outside was as cold and icy as she'd known it would be. He turned into the biting wind and they took a few steps. The water rushing by the moving boat was as flat and gray as the skies overhead. Icy gusts flattened her hair and snaked under the hem of her jacket and up her sleeves.

"I talked to Detective Reece," he said, gripping her arm as they slowly made headway. She positioned her head not only to hear him better but to protect her face. Her nose felt as if it was about to snap off. "He heard from Sergeant Jones down in Seaport." When she glanced up at him, the expression in his eyes warned her there was bad news in the offing. "Two beachcombers found a dead body last night—"

She gasped as her knees buckled.

He caught her. "No, honey, I'm sorry. Not Sabrina. It was a man. They've identified him as Hank Tyson."

Once she was able to speak again, she mumbled, "Who is Hank Tyson?"

"The hotel maintenance guy, the one who didn't come into work this weekend. Reece says he's been dead a couple of days."

"The poor guy," Sophie said, recovered now from her scare. "Did he get trapped by a wave or fall?"

"Reece says it appears he was strangled. It's still unclear if he died from that or the subsequent fall. They'll know more after the autopsy."

Sophie stared at him. "Murdered?"

"Yeah. Sophie, think about it. Hank didn't show up for work Saturday morning. What if someone killed him with the intention of taking his place? Then the hotel got their own employee to cover and he called in Brad Withers and his man Adam something... The thing is maybe the guy who stole Sabrina killed Hank."

"Or maybe Hank's brother-in-law or bookie or estranged wife settled a grudge," Sophie offered.

"True, but I don't like coincidences."

They'd reached the blunt-nosed end of the ferry. In the near distance, Sophie saw the lights and shapes of Weather Island drawing closer. Jack steered them around the corner where the wind was mercifully at their backs. "Why would this 'someone' choose Sabrina out of all the other women in the hotel, and more importantly, why would he kill a guy just on the chance he could snatch a victim in such a public place?" Sophie mused aloud.

"His target was Sabrina and no one else," Jack said, his voice tight. He ran his hand through his hair. "Remember that Sabrina saw someone painting her neighbor's porch. The next day she came home to the impression her house had been violated."

"Jack, what are you saying?"

"In addition to presumably Danny's half brother apparently leaving origami foxes outside her door, never indoors, by the way, there was also another man. This one took pictures of her while she was cooking." His eyes grew bright for a moment and Sophie knew all this was relating right back to Lisa, at least in his mind and his heart. "If he went inside her house and looked through her belongings, he could have seen she had reservations at the Seaport hotel."

Sophie's heart skipped a beat. "I saw scraps of papers on her desk. It appeared she'd jotted down pertinent information about her plans, including hotels and things like that." She stared at him a moment before adding, "You're talking two separate men with the same goal."

"No," he said quietly. "I'm talking two men with two different agendas. One—Danny's half brother, whose aim is to silence Sabrina for some unknown reason. His possible MO is leaving little foxes to intimidate her, throwing rocks in the attempt she'll fall off a cliff and it will look like an accident, trying to run her down. He's not very proficient. Even pointing a gun at you didn't work out. He's dangerous because he's desperate, again for some unknown reason, and his attempts are escalating in violence."

"And the other man?" she asked.

"This guy is different. This guy is a hunter and he's got Sabrina in his sights. For some reason, he fixated on her, spied on her with his camera, came into her house, looked at her things but didn't touch them, made her shudder when she couldn't even see him. And he killed to get to her."

"Jack, that's awful."

"Yeah. But the worst part is we know the half

brother doesn't have her or he wouldn't be trying to do in her look-alike—you. That means that this second guy—"

"Don't say it," Sophie blurted out, the ice shards racing through her body having nothing to do with the blustering weather. "You're talking about a cold-blooded killer, a beast, a man like the one who killed Lisa." Warm tears rolled down her frigid face. "You have to be wrong."

The ferry horn blast caught them both by surprise. Jack wrapped an arm tightly around her shoulders as the boat maneuvered its way to the pier.

Chapter Eight

"Being on this island seems like a giant waste of time," Sophie said as Jack followed his phone's voice directions to the Cannon estate. "We should be back in Oregon looking for Sabrina."

"We have three hours before the ferry returns for the trip back to Seattle," Jack reminded her. "And please, don't forget we're looking for the guy who tried to kill you—twice. Who knows, when questioned it might turn out he saw something that will help the police find Sabrina."

"Yeah, I know," Sophie said. "I'm just scared. You know, for her."

He squeezed her hand. "This morning," he said to distract her, "I asked Reece about both Danny's brother and this Cannon guy. He told me Danny's brother's legal name is Paul Rey. He just got out after serving three years for assault. Oh, and they're picking up Danny for questioning. As for Cannon, he's the force behind a lumber empire. It seems he's too rich for his own good."

"And Danny's mother works for him."

"Yep. Her name is Nora Rey. Fifty-five years old, has worked as his assistant slash gopher for umpteen years, trusted employee, etcetera."

"Raised two sons," Sophie added. "One criminal, one attorney with questionable ethics and motives."

"Yeah, well, what Danny told you about his father was only half-true. He did work on a ferry but not as the captain. He was a deckhand and he got fired from that job when he was caught stealing valuables out of passengers' vehicles. After that, he left the family and traveled to Alaska, where he was killed during a bar fight. Meanwhile, Nora married another loser, this one named George Reynard, and gave birth to son Paul. George killed two men in an alley during a robbery a year later. Apparently, she shortened her surname after his death, maybe so her young son wouldn't grow up with the stigma of his father's crimes."

He paused for a second, wanting to protect her feelings but knowing eventually she would learn the truth and it might be kinder coming from him. "Danny also lied to you about quitting his job in Seattle in order to move to Portland to marry you. He was actually terminated months ago because of suspected ethics violations. He's got a kind of…checkered…relationship with things like truth and honesty."

"So he wasn't a practicing attorney when he 'bumped into me' at the grocery store?"

"Nope."

"Boy, I sure want to know what he was up to. I hope his mom can tell me."

"We should find that out very soon," Jack said as the

phone announced they'd reached their destination. Jack slowed in front of open wrought iron gates flanking an uphill drive. He drove straight through and eventually they found themselves at the highest point on the island next to a large house that stood against the icy, gray skies like a Gothic nightmare.

"Yikes," Sophie said.

"No kidding." He stopped the car in front of the stairs leading to a flagstone porch and an arched doorway. As they hurried through the sleet to cover, it was impossible not to notice the 360-degree view that took in everything from the ferry landing far below, to Seattle's obscured skyline to the east.

Their knock was answered almost at once, making Jack wonder if there were surveillance cameras on the gates or warning sensors along the steep driveway.

The woman they faced looked worn-out. Gray hair cut blunt framed a heavily lined face decorated by a pair of bifocals.

The woman gaped at Sophie. "What are *you* doing here?" she all but whispered.

"You recognize me," Sophie said.

"No. Of course not." The absurdity of this response seemed to occur to her and she shook her head. "You're one of them."

"One of who?" Jack asked.

"Those damn twins. You have to be Sabrina."

"Why do you think I'm Sabrina?" Sophie asked.

"Because Sophia's with Dan—" She stopped abruptly and looked from one of them to the other. "Why *are* you here? How do you know—"

"Please," Jack said. "It's cold and wet. Let's not stand here talking in circles, okay? You're Nora, right?"

"Nora Rey, yes." The woman bit her pale bottom lip before standing aside and holding the door open. "You'd better come in."

The entry was two stories tall, dimly lit and oppressive. Steep stairs climbed to the next floor while a crystal-and-gilt unlit chandelier hung suspended from the ceiling. "Follow me," Nora said as she crossed to the threshold of a much smaller and more intimate room. She gestured for them to enter. Once they had, she followed them inside, closing the door behind her, her movements smooth and silent as though she'd spent her life gliding around this very large house like a wraith.

She turned to face Sophie. "Which one are you?"

"I'm Sophia Sparrow."

"I missed a call from Daniel last night. Was that about...you?"

"Probably. Mrs. Rey, Sabrina is missing. Jack and I are here because two days ago your son Danny asked me to be his wife. That same day, your son Paul tried to kill me. The police are actively seeking Paul for questioning concerning my attempted murder and the possible kidnapping of Sabrina."

"Murder! What in the world?"

"Paul tried to kill me," Sophie repeated. "He's still trying for that matter. We believe his intended victim is Sabrina but when she disappeared he mistook me for her."

"Oh, for heaven's sake," Nora interrupted, her thin

hand fluttering near her throat. "That boy! How did he find out about all this? What about Daniel? Are you two getting married? I mean, how could you resist such a fine man?"

"Easily!" Sophie said with enough horror in her voice to make Jack feel better about life. "Mrs. Rey, please explain all this to us."

"There's nothing to explain," she said, her lips compressed.

"Don't forget the police will be here sooner or later," Jack said.

"Oh, your damn grandfather," she said wearily with another glance at Sophie. "He's the one I blame."

"Both my grandfathers are dead," Sophie said.

"Not your genuine one, he's not dead, leastwise, not yet, though his time is running out, poor soul." Nora said this with a heavenward glance that Jack took to mean the old guy was tucked away somewhere upstairs.

Sophie backed up to a chair and sat down heavily. "He's here? In this house?" Nora's brief nod brought a groan from Sophie. "I've known something like this was coming since the moment I saw Sabrina's picture on your camera," she told Jack. Her dark eyes were round and stunned. "I don't know why I'm surprised."

"God, you look just like her," Nora said. "You even sound like her."

"Who?"

"Your mother. If the old man had just left things as they were."

"Stop talking in riddles," Jack said with a glance

at his watch. "We're running out of time here. By 'old man,' you mean R. H. Cannon?"

"The one in the same," Nora said as she sat down in a chair close to Sophie's. Jack remained standing, too impatient to get back to Oregon to even think about sitting. He could feel Sophie's nerves from three feet away as she leaned forward in her chair, her hands gripped between her knees.

The housekeeper smoothed a few wrinkles from her gray dress as she avoided looking at either one of them.

"Nora?" Jack prompted. "Tell Sophie about her mother and her grandfather. Help her understand."

"Please," Sophie added.

Nora looked up and sighed loudly. "I never wanted anybody to get hurt, I just wanted Danny to have what I couldn't give him on my own. But you deserve the truth. It started with his daughter, your mother. Her name was Shelly and she was as stubborn and head-strong as Mr. Cannon. When she turned up pregnant at sixteen, he threw her out. She showed up again a few months later, just about ready to pop and sick as a dog. He relented and she gave birth upstairs, right here in this house. She died the next day."

Nora shook her gray head. "What was he supposed to do with two infants? He didn't even want to see them so he had his attorney arrange private adoptions. He demanded all the papers be given to him, and those he destroyed because he never wanted to see those kids again, he wanted no path to lead back to him. Over the years, he hinted that me and my boys would inherit his wealth when he died. Who else did he have?"

"So Danny grew up thinking he would be well-off one day," Sophie said quietly. Jack could all but see the gears spinning in her head as she tried to merge the Danny she'd thought she knew with the actual man he was.

"Well-off? Ha. Rich is more like it. This house, the island, the millions in his bank account, everything. And Mr. Cannon liked the boys whenever they came with me to work. In those days I came back and forth to the island. Now I just live here full-time. Anyway, you know how little boys can be. Loud, clumsy, taking things that amuse them… Mr. Cannon had something of a short fuse. Things kind of went downhill as they got older."

"In what way?" Jack asked.

"The university Mr. Cannon helped Daniel get into threatened to expel him over another boy's claim that Daniel cheated on his exams. At first Mr. Cannon said he wouldn't help, but in the end he made a big grant and Daniel graduated. What's a couple of million to the old guy compared to my son's reputation? But Daniel had…issues…in law school. He was too clever for those dullards and they resented him. Right after that, Paul was arrested for some little thing he swears he didn't do. Mr. Cannon bailed them both out but he said he'd had enough, he wasn't going to help them again."

"Mrs. Rey," Jack said when she fell into thought, "it's getting late and we have a ferry to catch. Please get to the point."

"Oh, very well. Last fall, when Mr. Cannon's doctor told him he didn't have much time left, Mr. Cannon decided he wanted to see what had become of his granddaughters, so he hired a private detective to find them. After learning about how each had made something of themselves, at least in his book, he decided he wanted to see their faces, so he ordered photographs."

She looked at Sophie and shook her head. "You and your sister are spitting images of your mother. That got to the old man. He called his lawyer. I kind of overhead them discussing changing his will, you know, before the door was closed all the way. The end result was he cut both of my boys off, and left me a modest endowment. And after all I've done for him, the years I've dedicated—"

"He commissioned photographs," Jack said with a quickening pulse and a glance at Sophie. "That means someone took pictures of you and Sabrina."

"I never noticed anything," Sophie said.

"But Sabrina did. She caught the man on the neighbor's porch." He forced himself not to jump to conclusions. *Gather facts.* "How do you know what's in his will?" he asked Nora.

"He told me."

Sure, Jack thought. He'd bet that none of the old guy's mail got to him without first going through her. How many envelopes had she steamed open? Most likely she found the will and read it without anyone's knowledge. "What about the results of his investigation into his granddaughters' identities? Did he tell you about that, too?"

"The file was just lying around. I…happened to see it one day."

"And you told your sons," Sophie said.

"I told Daniel. It was his future at stake."

"And Paul?"

"I never said a word to Paul," she vowed.

"Why not? It's his future, too, isn't it?"

Nora produced a folded tissue that she used to dab at her dry eyes. Jack knew a delaying tactic when he saw one. "Nora?"

"Paul was…is…a problem. At first he was in jail and then when he got out he was so wired and unpredictable. Who could talk to him about anything—important? I mean, he took his father's full last name again like it was some badge of honor. Paul Reynard, big whoop. I even heard him refer to himself as 'The Fox.' That's what his dad called himself umpteen years before. Some fox. More like a chicken, killing those men by stabbing them in the back. Daniel always said his brother was a loose cannon and that's just how he was acting."

"Reynard is similar to the French word for *fox*, *renard*," Sophie said with a long glance at Jack. "As in those origami foxes he fashioned to threaten Sabrina."

"That fits what we know about him," Jack said.

"If Paul knows about you and Sabrina, then he learned it elsewhere," Nora volunteered. "After all, there was only one available girl." She added this last part with a sweeping glance at Sophie.

"So Danny told Paul and they cooked this scheme up between the two of them," Sophie said.

Nora looked aghast. "No. Daniel wouldn't say

a word to his brother. But Paul could have snooped around here while I was busy caring for Mr. Cannon."

"Do you know where Paul is now?" Jack asked.

She sniffed and shook her head. "No."

"You need to call him off."

"I have no way of doing that. He was here last week when the doctor told us that Mr. Cannon had taken a turn for the worse. The old geezer is dying, sooner rather than later. If Paul got it in his mind that he has to get rid of the other girl, well, that's what he'll try to do."

"What about the name and location of the investigator Mr. Cannon employed."

"How would I know?"

"Nora, I swear—"

"Okay, keep your pants on. Something Taylor. In Portland. That's all I know." She studied Sophie again. "I suppose you want to meet your grandfather. Let him see you in the flesh, cement your inheritance."

Sophie shook her head. "When this is all over, maybe Sabrina and I will come here and meet him—together."

"It might be too late by then," the housekeeper said.

For Jack, the words had an ominous ring to them on several fronts.

"So, Danny figured if he married me he would get at least half of my share of my grandfather's inheritance," Sophie said as they drew closer to her house in Portland. They'd each been wrapped in their own thoughts during the ferry ride back to Seattle and the subsequent drive south. Sophie knew that dealing with Danny was the easiest part of what was to come. It was her pending conversation with her mother that she dreaded.

"It looks that way."

"I wonder how he ever convinced himself that I wouldn't eventually see his true motives," she continued. "I mean, his family's connection to my grandfather is obvious—how could he not know I would figure it out? Didn't he learn anything in law school about grounds for annulment or divorce? How dumb and naive did he think I was?"

Jack shrugged, which considering his options seemed like the better part of valor, even to Sophie. Instead he offered an observation of his own. "I think Paul decided that since Sabrina was already married and therefore unlikely to marry someone new before your grandfather died that killing her would mean everything would go to you and thus Danny. Then Paul could show up and have a private chat with his half brother where he could point out how helpful he'd been and claim his share."

"What a couple of morons," Sophie said. "And we're still no closer to finding Sabrina."

Jack reached across the gearshift and took her hand. "Sophie, you know I called Detective Reece on the ferry ride back to Seattle, right?"

"I overheard you," she admitted. "I take it Danny got himself all lawyered-up and that Paul is still on the run."

"Reece also contacted Kyle Woods's grandfather up in Canada. The man swears his grandson hasn't been up there to see him since Christmas and that he's not expecting him until his birthday bash in March. They also checked with Homeland Security. Woods's car hasn't crossed the border. In other words, Kyle is also missing."

"Are the police connecting Sabrina and him?"

"Unofficially, yes. Since Sabrina's car hasn't been seen since Saturday, they're pretty sure she's off with Kyle somewhere on a lover's tryst. And they're very happy with Paul Rey, aka Reynard as the man behind everything else, including Hank Tyson's murder down in Seaport."

"Did they find Mr. Tyson's vehicle?"

"Yeah, at his house. Apparently he was killed there and dumped on that beach."

"So they're not operating on the theory Sabrina has been kidnapped."

"Reece says the chief needs proof before he starts messing with Sabrina's Fourth Amendment right against unreasonable search and seizure. We need something to demonstrate she's in some sort of danger."

"And gut feelings aren't enough."

"No. Especially since I don't know her well and you've never met her at all. But don't worry, I'm going to find your grandfather's detective tonight and get the names of the people who photographed you and Sabrina. If the chief needs proof, I'll get it for him. Do you want to come with me?"

What she wanted was Sabrina, and the desire to meet her, to see her, to touch her was so overwhelming that it took her breath away. But with the very next breath, something else happened. One minute she was riding along in a warm car. The next she was running for her life, plunging through the dark, desperate and terrified.

And then a roar like a mountain lion thundered through her head. Giant teeth closed over her leg, pierced her skin, pulled her to the ground, dragged her back into the underbrush, into oblivion. The putrid smell of rot filled her nostrils as dirty cold water splashed over her face.

The despair was as unbearable as the pain.

Sophie opened her mouth to scream but as suddenly as these sensations had dominated her mind and body they were gone.

Jack's hand brushed hers. "Are you okay?"

"Yeah. Fine," she said with a shaky voice. If what she'd just experienced was a glimpse into Sabrina's soul it meant she was alive, but only just. With a surge of passion, Sophie wished she could join her sister wherever she was, for how did a person fight such desperation alone?

"You got awfully quiet."

"Maybe we've got this all wrong," she said slowly. "Maybe Sabrina drove off the road and is lying in a ditch somewhere out of sight." Trapped and hurt in a mangled car would certainly account for the cold, the water, the hopelessness, especially after two nights alone.

"The police searched the highways."

"Which highways? North, south, east? The only direction she couldn't have driven was west into the ocean. They can't possibly have searched every single side road. For heaven's sake, she's a firefighter. Why don't we get her coworkers all up and down the coast to help look for her? Isn't that what they do, save people?"

"Good idea."

"We need to go back to Astoria."

"I know. But I have to talk to the PI first. I need the names of the photographers. I can't operate solely on the supposition she's been in a car crash."

"I know you can't," Sophie said. "You go do the detective thing, I'll do the mom thing, then we can drive to Astoria together."

Warmth spread up her arm as he took her hand. "That sounds good. I don't want to be far away from you."

"I don't want that either," she said, and an understanding of some sort traveled between them.

"I'll let you off at your house and then come back for you." He added, "And, Sophie, if you feel the need to stay in Portland for the night, we can do that."

She raised his hand to her face, held his knuckles against her cheek and kissed his fingers. Maybe she'd known him less than three days, but they'd been three pretty intense days and no matter what her head said about falling in love, she suspected her heart had a mind of its own. "I'll be ready when you come back for me," she said as she got out of the car and watched him drive away.

"You're back," Margaret Sparrow said as Sophie walked into the house. Her mother sat on her recliner as always. Oscar lay on her lap but he sprang to his feet when he saw Sophie and scampered to her side.

She knelt down to scoop the cat into her arms, sparing a second to wonder if Sabrina's tabby, Gabby, was okay. Tomorrow, she'd go get the cat from the vet's. Tomorrow, with any luck, they would find Sabrina and she would finally meet her twin sister.

"I haven't heard from Danny," her mother said with pursed lips. "I think you blew it."

Sophie sat down on the sofa. "Never mind Danny." She took a deep breath, aware that she might not have very long before Jack returned. "I know what happened," she added.

"You know what exactly?" her mother scoffed and Sophie stared hard at her a second. Had she always been this antagonistic and sour? Pretty much, Sophie realized. She wasn't sure what had triggered such negativity—for most of her life she'd assumed she'd been the cause, that disappointment in her only child or even the fact that she hadn't wanted a child in the first place had made Sophie an unbearable burden.

But now, looking at the woman who had raised her, who had nurtured her in her own way…well, she wasn't sure about anything.

Maybe that was where to start this conversation. "I know I'm adopted," she said. "I know I have a twin sister and I know who my biological grandfather is. What I'd like to know from you is how it all began, for you and Dad, I mean." She took a deep breath. How could she ask her mother to be honest if she couldn't do the same, even with herself? "What I'm asking you, Mom, is this—was there ever a point where *you* loved me?"

Her mother looked at her defiantly.

I'm wasting my time, Sophie thought as Oscar jumped off her lap and headed to the kitchen.

Sophie looked from the cat's retreating form to her mother's face. Were those tears glittering in the older woman's eyes?

IT WAS LATE afternoon by the time Jack found Dominick Taylor Investigations. The downtown building he entered was a converted three-story house divided into separate offices. A sign directed Jack to the basement.

At the bottom of the stairs he found a glass door printed with the investigator's name and he tried the knob, hoping it would turn, hoping the guy hadn't gone home for the day.

It was locked. He rapped his knuckles against the glass. "Anyone here?" he called.

It took a second, but then he heard approaching footsteps. The door was opened by a man twice his age whose once dark hair was now threaded with white. He wore thick glasses, but behind the lenses, the eyes were bright and curious. Suspenders held up faded jeans and he was in the process of shrugging on a tweed sports coat. "I'm just on my way out," he said. "Think you can come back tomorrow?"

"I'm afraid not," Jack said and showed him his own license, explaining in as succinct of terms as possible who he was. He threw in Cannon's name as an incentive for cooperation. "I hate to sound dramatic, but it could very well be a matter of life and death," he ended.

The man stepped aside. "Dominick Taylor, call me Dom," the man said, gesturing to his desk, where he indicated Jack should take a seat in the visitor's chair. He settled himself in his own worn swivel chair, the seat sagging, the armrest wrapped in duct tape. A large computer sat off to one side, much as it did on Jack's own desk back in California.

"I've never actually met Cannon," Dom said. "His attorneys contacted me."

"He wanted to find out the identity of his grand-daughters," Jack said.

Dom nodded but with obvious hesitation. Jack understood the old guy was determined to protect his client and his coworkers and he respected that. "That investigation had to be tricky," he said. "I was told by Cannon's housekeeper of many years that he had destroyed all the records of his granddaughters' adoptions. In fact, I got the impression he'd never even known the adopted family's names."

"That's what I was told," Dom said. "Hard to believe, isn't it? I have three little grandkids of my own— well, everyone is different. Anyway the lawyer he used was long dead, his office long gone. But we finally found a secretary who remembered the event because... well, suffice to say she remembered it."

"Because it separated identical twin babies," Jack stated, "and I bet that got to her."

Dom smiled. "You're right, it did. She confessed she'd thought many times over the years that she'd like to tell them about each other. In the end, she kept her word and didn't say anything."

"The cat is out of the bag now," Jack said. "Sophia knows about Sabrina and, if at all possible, she will soon tell Sabrina their story. That's why I'm here, to make sure they have a chance at long last to meet."

"Did their grandfather tell them about each other or did they find out through their pending inheritance?"

"Neither. Sabrina is my buddy's wife and she asked for help because she felt threatened. Her twin sister, Sophie, happened to show up at the same hotel. I mistook her for Sabrina. Together, we discovered Sabrina is missing. The police think they have it all wrapped up but I have a horrible suspicion they're set on the wrong man."

"What do you need from me?" Dom asked as he picked up a pencil and started doodling eyes on a piece of paper.

"I was told the dossier was to include photographs taken on the sly of each woman."

"I took Sophia's myself," Dom said and, swiveling the chair, opened the bottom drawer of a tall cabinet and withdrew a fat file. He took out two photographs. The top one was of Sophie taken as she left a school, obviously, the one at which she taught. Her hair was lighter, longer, and one hand was raised as if to sweep it away from her face. She wore boots and a brown coat buttoned up to her chin. She looked downtrodden somehow, timid, not much like the woman he'd gotten to know the last few days and nothing like the image he carried of her in his heart.

Sophia. His Sophie. Face it, that's how he thought of her, as his. Crazy.

"This one was taken by a guy in Astoria," Dom said, shuffling the photographs around. "I met him once at a friend's place. Funny guy. Anyway, when I couldn't leave town to go to Astoria myself, I sent him directions." He slid a photograph forward.

Sabrina's photo was a three sixty from Sophia's. It had been taken through what appeared to be her kitchen window, the lens zoomed into her face. He could see the steam rising around her, even a few moist droplets on her brow and sticking to the dark tendrils of her hair.

"Arty, isn't it?" Dom said.

"She told me about this," Jack told him. "She felt violated by the photographer."

"She saw him?"

"Yes. He posed as a painter."

Dom's lips disappeared as he frowned. "I wondered how he got something so…personal. The instructions were to get a shot like that of the other girl, a head-to-toe, but this is all he sent me."

"I need his name," Jack said.

"I feel funny giving it to you," Dom said quietly.

"Look, he probably has nothing to do with nothing. But maybe he saw someone else when he was looking at her, who knows? I'm not the cops. They don't even seem to think she's in trouble. I'll make sure he doesn't connect you with me but I have to talk to him and I don't have time to interview every photographer in Astoria."

"Be that as it may…" Dom said with obvious hesitation.

Jack cleared his throat, ever aware of the time ticking away and the urgency of the situation. "Let me put it this way, Dom. Cannon wanted to leave his grand-daughters his fortune because somewhere in his heart he knew he hadn't done right by them. The last thing in the world he'd want is to harm them because of something he instigated. From what I hear he's on his deathbed. I don't have time to go back to Weather Island and get him to sign a release form or whatever. It's up to you and me to use our heads."

Dom folded his hands under his chin and narrowed his eyes. At last he said, "Louis. Louis Nash. I don't know how much work he does, what with that limp of his. I don't know where he lives—we did everything over the internet."

"Limp?" Jack asked as alarm stepped up his heart-beat.

"Yeah."

"Which leg?"

"Let me think. The right. Maybe. I only met him once and then I only saw him take a step or two. Yeah, right. I think. Sorry. Does it matter?"

"Probably not," Jack said, but he was already call-ing up Lisa's file that he kept on his phone. He found the composite sketch he was looking for and showed it to Dom. "Is this him?"

Dom made a cursory glance. "Nah, Louis is over forty. This guy is what? Twentysomething?"

"It's a ten-year-old drawing," Jack pointed out and felt foolish. There was no way Lisa's killer and this man could be one and the same. Lots of people limped and not all limps were chronic.

Dom took the phone and studied the screen, then

handed it back. "Sorry. I mean, it could be. Louis is tall, thinner than that sketch, older—I can't tell. But sketches—I mean, really, they all kind of look alike. Who is this guy?"

"A killer," Jack said quickly.

"Nah, not Louis. He's not the type."

"Chances are good you're right," Jack said as he met Dom's gaze head-on. He knew he'd jumped to conclusions when he heard about the photographer's limp and was already regretting casting aspersions on a man who might very well be as innocent as the driven snow. "That said," he added, "you and I both know there's no way to look inside another man's soul."

"No," Dom said with a weary sigh. "No, there's not."

Chapter Nine

"How long did Lisa live after she was abducted?" Sophie asked Jack as they drove the dark twisting road to the coast. Her question was met with silence but she had to know. "Jack?"

"The condition of her burned body made it difficult to tell for sure," he finally said.

"It's been three days for Sabrina," Sophie whispered almost to herself.

"Remember the cases aren't related," Jack said. "Even if Sabrina's been abducted, it's extremely unlikely it's by the same guy. The odds are astronomical."

"But you showed the investigator Lisa's killer's composite sketch. Doesn't that mean you've connected the two men?"

"Not in any concrete way," he said. "Lots of people limp. No one knows whether the guy who took Lisa had a chronic limp or an injury or maybe no limp at all. Maybe he just used it as a decoy thing. It just hit me hard when Dom mentioned his Astoria photographer limped. I let it get to me."

"Did you have a chance to talk to Detective Reece again? Have they apprehended Paul Rey?"

"I did talk to him briefly. He said they found Rey's car abandoned up in the woods. It's assumed he somehow got another. And that means you're still not safe, damn it. Oh, and Reece said he's talked to the fire department, who have decided to launch a thorough search of side roads starting tomorrow morning. Of course, Sabrina could still be in the Seaport area or have driven south, so those areas need to be searched, too. Search parties are being formed even as we speak."

"Now if we can just get the police to come around. Did you tell Reece about the photographer?"

"No," he said quickly. "I'll go talk to the guy first thing tomorrow. I don't want to cause Louis Nash trouble if he hasn't earned it."

"But how will you know?"

He shook his head. "You make a point. But we need Reece to take Sabrina's situation seriously. I can't afford to put him off by sounding like I'm hell-bent on revenge for a ten-year-old murder case that happened a thousand miles away."

Sophie sighed. "And the clock just keeps ticking."

"I know."

She drew quiet as she tried to reestablish a connection to Sabrina's psyche—if that's what had happened earlier when she "felt" the raindrops and smelled the dirt—but had no luck.

"Tell me what happened with your mother," Jack said. She was startled out of her thoughts, but she knew he was trying to divert her attention and she appreciated it.

"She started out defensive but eventually opened up," Sophie reported. "In fact, I think it's the only genuine conversation she and I have ever had."

"That's good, right?"

"Yeah, it is. She told me how she and Dad had been turned down by various adoption agencies because of their health. When their friend—who was an attorney—heard about this private no-questions-asked adoption, they jumped on it. I think most people would have been a little put off by the fact that, technically speaking, it wasn't legal let alone ethical, but they saw it as a last chance for parenthood. Much to my surprise, Mom said she was as anxious as Dad to have a family."

"What happened to her…enthusiasm?" Jack asked.

"According to her, I gravitated toward Dad from the get-go. She also admitted she was nervous, always ready for my 'real' parents to demand me back. See, they had no idea where I came from, whose child I was, knew nothing about my grandfather or another baby. I think she decided it would be easier to lose me if she didn't get too attached."

"So she didn't know your grandfather was Mr. Moneybags."

"No idea. She's thrilled, by the way. In fact, she now says she never liked Danny, claims that I can do better."

"And what do you think?"

She slid him a long glance. "I think she's right, I *can* do better."

"Damn straight," he said with a charming grin that

lightened her heart for a moment as they drove into Astoria. Without discussing it, he drove straight to the Cromwell house. They found it as they'd left it: dark and seemingly empty. Just to be sure, Jack darted through the rain to knock. When he got back into the car, he took a deep breath. "I think we might as well have dinner and get a good night's sleep. What do you think?"

"Sounds good."

The hotel Jack checked them into was built on the site of a former fish cannery and boasted a restaurant of its own. They both ordered scallops and shared a bottle of Pinot Gris. All around them, people dining by candlelight seemed engaged in intimate conversations as they enjoyed the good food and fine ambiance. But while there was no one in the world Sophie would rather share a meal with, she couldn't help but be preoccupied and she knew Jack was, too.

Would she ever meet the sister with whom she'd entered the world? The fear she would lose her on the eve of finding her was so strong as to border on a premonition. It was a relief when Jack set aside his napkin. "Let's get out of here," he said, and managed to reassure her with a smile.

They tried taking a walk, but the cold rain just made Sophie more upset. Was Sabrina outside in this and hurt? Both tired and heartsick, they retreated to their room, where Sophie told Jack to take the first shower as she had finally remembered to bring clothes of her own from home and needed to sort what she'd hastily thrown in the suitcase.

When it was her turn to bathe, she soaked in the huge tub before changing into the only silky night garment she owned, a long gown that almost matched the fading lilac streak in her hair.

Jack whistled as she reentered the room. "I thought I would miss seeing you in my oversize plaid flannel pajama top, but wowza, you look gorgeous."

She pirouetted. "Thank you."

He was propped up in bed fooling with his phone. He set it beside the lamp, tossed open the covers and held out an arm. "Come here," he coaxed and she crawled in beside him. He gathered her into his arms and held her so close his heart seemed to beat for her, too.

For a second they stared into each other's eyes.

"You look so sad it's breaking my heart," he whispered as he touched her cheek.

"I'm sorry."

"You don't need to be." He hugged her tighter. "She's never far away from my mind either, and now I heard from Buzz. He's in New Zealand and he's worried sick because Sabrina isn't responding to his calls or email. I told him she's still off on her own. God, I have to find her before he gets here the day after tomorrow. And not just for him either."

"For Lisa and for yourself," she whispered against his wonderfully bare muscular chest.

"No, Sophie, for you. I have to get her home safely for you." He lifted her chin and met her gaze. "Don't you know that?"

Tears filled her eyes and rolled down her cheeks as

she nodded. He held her even tighter. The musky scent of his skin seemed to envelop her, while the physical strength of his arms surged strength of another kind into her bones.

"If she's off romancing fireman Kyle, I'm going to be really pissed off," he added.

"She's not off romancing anyone," Sophie said with 100 percent certainty.

"How can you be so sure?"

She closed her eyes and thought about how to respond. In the end she simply said, "I just am. She needs us."

"You can feel her?" he asked.

"Kind of. I just know that she was alive around five o'clock. But she's hurt and scared and about to give up hope." She cast him an upward glance. "We have to find her tomorrow, Jack, we just have to."

He kissed her lips and her forehead. "We will," he said with confidence ringing in his voice.

She closed her eyes, reaching inward, outward, just trying to stay open to any sensation, but there was nothing there. Just the steady beat of Jack's heart reverberating throughout her body.

And for now, that would have to be enough.

JACK WOKE UP with a start. He thought someone was rattling the door and for a second his body tensed. Sophie still lay in his arms, her lovely face visible thanks to a wash of light that fell across the bed. The sound came again and he realized it was the wind blowing a chair against the outside wall of their balcony.

As if sensing his tenseness, her eyes fluttered open. "Is it morning?" she mumbled.

"It's the middle of the night," he told her, burying his head in her fragrant hair, kissing her petal-soft neck. She turned her head and his lips found hers.

What happened next was like being swept up by a giant wave, tossed around in tumultuous fury until finally being thrown onto a foreign beach. They tore at each other's clothes, desperate for the feel of each other, kissing and exploring as they went until they came together with an inevitable explosion. It was over in a flash and they lay side by side, both breathing heavy, Sophie's lovely gown a heap on the floor along with his pajama bottoms. Everything was the same and yet totally different. He couldn't keep from touching her, enjoying the weight of her breasts in his hands and the dewy softness of her rounded buttocks. She, too, explored his body until at last their caresses awakened the same burning hunger that once again brought them together.

Jack had had lovers over the years, some more serious than others, none since Lisa whom he'd ever seriously contemplated a future with, but this was different. He wasn't positive how. He only knew some meals you ate with relish and walked away from the table, sated. And some meals were so special you lingered and then yearned to indulge yourself again, and again.

"That was like a firestorm," Sophie whispered against his ear as her fingers twined in his hair.

He tightened his arm to bring her closer. "I thought of a tidal wave."

She giggled sleepily, the sound like a trilling brook. A trilling brook? Good heavens, he was obviously under her spell. A smile curved his lips as his consciousness drifted away like a wisp of smoke.

"It's too early for room service," Jack said as he stared at the room's complimentary coffee machine. He lifted a packet of what promised to be a Hawaiian blend of deeply roasted beans—sure, he thought—and added, "I'll just double up the packets."

There was no way in the world Sophie wanted to lift the lid on another room service tray until Paul Rey was behind bars, so she simply nodded. She'd dressed in clean jeans, a thermal undershirt and wool sweater and now laced up a pair of hiking boots. The final touch was a pair of silver earrings that she'd grabbed off her dresser at home. Belatedly she recalled Danny had given them to her, but she put them on anyway. The elongated silver discs caught the light and brightened her face.

"You look great," Jack said and she caught his reflection staring at her image in the mirror. "Nice earrings."

She turned. "Thanks. Danny bought them for me."

He shook his head and approached her, wrapping his

hands around her waist and kissing her lips. "I could have gone all day without knowing that."

She laughed. "I picked them out."

"Good."

"Hmm—"

They drank a hurried cup of coffee that was still too weak before leaving the hotel room Sophie knew she would always remember. They emerged into a dry morning, holding hands.

And therein lay the conundrum. Sophie felt as if her soul was torn in two. On one hand, she'd never been this happy in her life. Jack was a fantastic lover, generous and thoughtful, yet powerful and assertive. Being special to him made her heart burst. But Sabrina was going on four days of missing and that same joyous heart knew with certainty that time was running out.

They stuffed their things into the trunk before Jack clicked the doors open. Sophie was about to open the passenger door when she saw a small plastic opaque bag tied to the handle.

"Someone was out late or up early distributing something or the other," she said, glancing at the cars parked close by, looking for similar yellow bags. There were none. Jack showed up at her side, and for a second they both stared at the cheerful bag, feeling anything but cheerful.

"Do you want me to open it?" he asked.

"No, I'll do it. I even have gloves in my pocket." She pulled on her gloves and opened the string. They both peered inside and, to no one's surprise, found themselves looking at an origami fox folded from a dollar bill.

"He's back," Sophie said.

Jack grabbed the bag from her hand. "Get in the car, honey. We're going to go visit Detective Reece."

"WE'VE GOT EVERY available man working on finding that nutcase," Reece reported as he sent the yellow bag with its contents off to the lab. He poured them each a cup of coffee from his personal pot. The brew was so strong it reminded Jack of the stuff they used to drink back when he was a cop in LA. Some of the guys had complained it took the enamel off their teeth. Jack had liked it just fine.

"Paul Rey must have been here the whole time, watching Sabrina's house," Jack said. "We drove there right after arriving back in Astoria last night, then went to the hotel, where we parked in their lot. As you know, it's unfenced."

Reece's cherubic smile faded. "I'll set up a watch on the Cromwell house." He dug in his cabinet and withdrew a file that he laid on his desk and opened. "This is what the loser looks like," he said, turning the photo so they could see it. Paul Rey was about thirty in his prison mug shot and like every other man Jack had seen in an orange jumpsuit, the color didn't become him. His blondish-red hair was cut very short, his mouth was set in a grim line and his eyes looked small and mean.

"He looks like Danny, only younger and a lot nastier," Sophie said.

"You're talking about Danny Privet," the detective said. "I talked to a friend in the Portland bureau. He says Danny is a slick piece of work."

"Yeah, but he's not as smart as he thinks he is," Jack said and Sophie nodded.

Reece turned the file back around. "By the way, Seattle police have questioned their mother, Nora Rey. She admits she told her older son Daniel about the inheritance but not Paul. More important, she claims she doesn't know how to reach him to call off his continued attacks on you, Ms. Sparrow."

"Well, so far he hasn't been real successful and now thanks to his latest origami fox, we know he's in town. Not the most subtle of stalkers." She got to her feet. "I want to join the hunt for Sabrina's car," she said with a glance at the wall clock.

"They've divided into several small groups with each unit tackling a road that leads out of town. It's a long shot they'll find anything but I understand your concern. Try driving out to River Bend. They're combing the verges of a road that connects over to Highway 30 and from there to Interstate 5 and just about anywhere else you want to go. You'll be relieved to know the firehouse in Seaport and all points south for that matter are organizing similar searches."

"Great. Come on, Jack."

Before he could respond, the detective spoke up. "Just a minute now, I have another request of you two.

I was wondering if you would mind going through Sabrina's house again. The chief says if we can rule out a clandestine tryst with Kyle Woods we can rev up the search. Maybe you can find something in that house that will give us a definitive clue about her relationship with the guy and this time look for anything that might suggest Sabrina came back home after you saw her in Seaport."

"Have you been checking to see if her phone or credit cards are being used or if she made an inordinate number of calls to Kyle before last weekend?" Sophie asked.

"We can't subpoena records without an investigation," Reece said. "But rest assured we're keeping an eye out for Woods, too. You have to admit it's odd for two 'friends' and coworkers to disappear at the same time, one with a false story about visiting a grandfather and the other while her husband is out of the country and neither of them using their phones or credit cards, neither one's vehicle being noticed...nothing."

"Then why would she call me?" Jack said.

"Who better to alibi whatever story she concocts than her hubby's best friend?"

"You've got this all wrong," Jack insisted.

"And all that aside, you have to keep in mind if she's been abducted she's in mortal danger," Sophie added. "Tell him about Lisa, Jack. Tell him about the photographer."

Sophie sat back down and the detective leaned his

forearms on his desk, poised to listen. "Who's Lisa?" he asked.

"An old friend, abducted and subsequently murdered ten years ago down in LA," he said. He explained the situation as he had to Sophie a day or so before.

"So what's the tie-in with Sabrina Cromwell? You didn't even know her then, did you?"

"No. Buzz hadn't met her yet. The only tie-in is the way she disappeared so suddenly and the fact that she was photographed cooking." He explained about Sophie's grandfather's hiring a private detective to assemble dossiers on each of his granddaughters and to include photographs of them. "Sophie's photo was taken by a guy in Portland. It's a standard head-to-toe shot of her leaving the school where she teaches. Sabrina's picture is sensual in nature." Jack paused to hand the detective Dominick's card with his name and address printed on it. "This is the investigator R. H. Cannon hired. He mentioned the photographer he engaged here in Astoria had a noticeable limp."

"Wait a second," the detective said as he studied Dom's card. "Are you talking about Louis?"

"Louis Nash," Jack said. "Do you know him?"

"He takes photographs here in town. Took my son's graduation picture, my daughter's, too. Nice guy. Pays his bills, supports his homebound mother, meets his obligations…never had one complaint against him."

"Then you know him?"

"I've met him. You're barking up the wrong tree."

"How long has he lived here?"

"Near as I can figure, his whole life."

"Was he ever in California?"

"I don't know, Jack."

"Have you had any missing women here in the last ten or fifteen years, maybe longer?"

"Are you accusing Louis Nash of—"

"I'm not accusing him of anything. I'm just asking."

"Well, the answer is the only unsolved murder of a young woman I know of happened years ago. Popular consensus is her boyfriend killed her and no, he wasn't Louis Nash. Listen, I see the guy around town all the time. He's not real chatty, but he's always polite."

Jack brought up the composite sketch of Lisa's suspected killer on his phone. "Does he look anything like this given the fact that the sketch was made ten years ago?"

The detective studied it just as Dom had. "Kind of. So do a hundred other guys. Is this the—"

"The man police suspect killed Lisa and at least one other woman. No one has ever identified him."

Reece shook his head. "You're on a crusade."

"I was afraid you'd think that but the truth is, I'm just trying to find Sabrina. Won't you at least ask Nash about taking her photograph? We know he trespassed on a neighbor's porch pretending to be a painter in order to get the shot he ultimately sent Dominick Taylor. Isn't trespassing enough cause to question him, even unofficially if that's as far as you're willing to go?"

"If the neighbor comes in here and files a complaint—"

"Detective, come on. Can't you just talk with him?"

Reece sighed, glanced at Sophie and ran a hand through his gray hair. "Yeah, okay, I can do that but it's not going to do you any good. I don't for a minute think a guy making a living by taking someone's photograph has a thing to do with anything—I think Paul Rey is the culprit. I think he killed the janitor down in Seaport to get at Sabrina. She must have run off to meet up with her boyfriend when he wasn't looking, but then Sophie shows up out of the blue. He mistakes her for her twin sister. And here we are."

"You're basing this whole thing on Sabrina willingly leaving Seaport of her own volition. But what if she didn't?" Jack argued. "We agree Paul Rey's motive for targeting Sabrina is to eliminate her before her grandfather dies and leaves her half a fortune, right?"

"Right."

"If he has her, if heaven forbid he's already killed her, then why go after Sophie? He'd have to know she isn't Sabrina."

"But he knows there are twins," Reece said. "Maybe he figures if both of the girls are dead, Cannon will leave all his dough to his loyal housekeeper and her two loser sons."

Jack had to admit that was a remote possibility. Rey wasn't the sharpest tool in the shed. "I appreciate the fact that you're willing to talk to Nash," he said with a reluctant nod. "I'll call you later and find out what you learn."

Sophie got to her feet. "After I finish the search I'll

go through the house again as you requested. By the way, did you get the test results back on the food off the tray?"

"The lab hasn't responded yet," Reece said. "What with it being a holiday weekend, I don't expect we'll hear back before Friday."

Jack knew what Sophie was thinking because he thought it, too.

By Friday, Sabrina would either be safe in her house with her cat and her husband or she would be dead.

Chapter Ten

Much of the land surrounding Astoria consisted of rivers and coastal plains, but it quickly changed as you traveled inland. Jack and Sophie soon found themselves driving steep, twisty country roads abutted with forests. Occasionally a dirt driveway fronted with a mailbox would announce a home existed somewhere out of sight but mainly it was lonely, desolate-looking countryside that was probably quite beautiful if not seen through the lens of unbearable worry.

They finally found the search already in progress and parked. Before they were completely out of the car, Sue jogged up to them. She was dressed in jeans and boots, like Sophie. Red frizz escaped from under the cap of a Portland Trailblazers cap.

"I saw you drive up," she said by way of greeting. "I wanted to talk to you."

"Sure," Sophie said. "What's up?"

It took Sue a second to speak, during which she stared at her feet and then at them. "I think I was a little flippant concerning Sabrina the other day," she finally said.

Sophie shook her head. "I wouldn't worry about it. You were just telling us things as you saw them."

"Yeah, well, the ugly truth is that after Barbara left Kyle I thought he and I might get together."

"Barbara is Kyle's wife?" Jack asked.

"Yeah. Anyway, it turns out Kyle only wanted to be around Sabrina. They had this bond… I guess they knew each other in high school. Face it, I got jealous. I mean she's got a smart, gorgeous husband and she looks like a movie star—why does she need Kyle, too? Anyway, when the police questioned me and I thought about what I'd insinuated about the two of them to you guys, well, I regretted it. I'm really sorry I was so snotty about the possibility Sabrina would walk away from a friend. I want to do whatever I can to help her."

"Then you don't think she's off with Kyle?"

"I guess it's possible but it seems unlikely she'd ask for your help and then abandon you like that."

"I agree," Jack said.

"I'm glad you told us," Sophie told Sue with a gentle squeeze of her arm.

Sue peered closely at her. "You look so much like Sabrina, but you're different, too."

"She's working on developing an edge," Jack said, nudging Sophie's side.

Sophie laughed. "He's right, I am. Anyway, Sabrina and I are identical twins but we were raised apart. We're bound to have our differences."

Sue nodded. "Come join our side of the road. All we've found so far, thank goodness, are a few unfortunate smashed critters and enough garbage to fill a swimming pool."

The terrain was heavily wooded and steep. On one side of the narrow road a shallow ravine climbed uphill and on the other the land dropped precipitously to a tributary river below that was all but invisible given the density of the foliage. In full winter rainy season, the sound of rushing water rumbled in the background.

The odd thing for Sophie was that she knew from about the second step she took along the south side of the road that they were close. Sabrina was near, she could almost feel it in her bones… What she couldn't feel was in what state her twin might be. Hurt, scared, alive, heaven forbid, dead… Sophie had no idea but the feeling that she was close was as real as the dirt beneath her feet.

A ticking bomb replaced her heartbeat.

"Jack, listen, I have to tell you something," she said, and whispered in his ear. "I sense Sabrina is close by."

"Are you sure?"

"It's just a feeling. Not the first I've had and maybe not real at all."

"Then we'll keep looking, okay?"

She nodded and matched him step for step, studying the roadside for tire tracks and broken branches—anything that would suggest a vehicle had left the road and tumbled out of sight.

"Here, over here!" someone called and along with everyone else, Sophie and Jack darted ahead to join a group staring downhill at the disturbed terrain running down toward the river before vanishing into a tangle of underbrush. Tire prints in the mud beside the road were indistinct at best.

"Okay, folks, listen up," a burly guy of about thirty said as he joined them. "You all know me, I'm Captain Philips with the Astoria division. We all know this is an informal search but just in case…fan out at arm's length and go down the slope, but not directly on this path. We don't want to destroy any evidence. If you see anything, mark it with one of the flags I gave you, and for good measure, stay there with whatever it is you found. Move slowly and watch where you step."

Sophie stood between Sue and Jack, nerves skittering over her skin like a thousand little ant bites as they started their descent. What if Sabrina's car was down here and Sabrina was beyond saving?

But there was another fear and that was that someone might have dumped Sabrina's body down here after torturing her and murdering her. They might even have burned her remains like Lisa's. How did you steel yourself for such a possibility?

She searched her mind and heart for some reassuring feeling that this wasn't the case, but whatever brief connection she thought she'd felt to her sister would not come back and she was as much in the dark as everyone else.

She glanced up in time to see Jack studying her. He took her hand and held it tightly in his.

The smell reached them halfway down the slope. Rotting flesh, she thought, and her stomach lurched. Jack's hand turned into the only thing keeping her from floating away, from escaping this moment.

"It looks like a four-wheel-drive vehicle came down here and backed up or something," Jack said softly. "The ground is all torn up."

"Jack, the smell—"

"Hold on, don't go imagining things," he said. They all stopped when the thicket in front of them became the last barrier to what was beyond.

"Yikes, what's that smell?" someone asked.

Someone else produced a machete and began whacking at the thicket, pushing it aside. Sophie saw a large shape emerging, rust and white paint. Her heart caught in her throat as Jack whispered, "Oh, God, is that Buzz's old Blazer?" She held her breath as the first of the branches fell.

It was not a Blazer and while Buzz's car might be old, this one was far older. It was also not alone. An old washing machine lying on its side and various car parts along with a rusty roll of chicken wire and an old toilet sporting a bowl full of weeds accompanied it.

And the cause of the smell was explained by a freshly butchered carcass.

"Oh, man, somebody poached a deer and cleaned it out here," Sue said.

"Everybody return to the road," the deputy said. "Same rules, watch where you step. I'm going to make sure a dead deer is all we got going on down here."

Jack grabbed Sophie's arms and turned her to face him. "I'll help the deputy. Go back up to the road with Sue, okay?"

"Yeah," Sophie said, glad to be told to leave this spot. "Okay."

Having found nothing else at the dump site, they returned to the search, but after another fruitless hour in which they discovered more cast-off debris but nothing to suggest Sabrina had ever come this way, Jack and Sophie left.

"I'm driving to Seaport," Jack said.

Sophie glanced at the dashboard clock, then in her rearview mirror. It would be so easy if she still felt that sensation of Sabrina's closeness. Then she could insist they return. As it was, there was no point, no feeling, no nothing.

"Shouldn't we search Buzz and Sabrina's house like the detective asked?"

"If we have time," he said. "I think he was giving us busywork. He's got a whole squad of people who can do that job. His mind may be made up or his hands tied, but mine aren't and neither are yours. I want to talk to the people at the hotel again."

"I could go to Sabrina's house while you do that," Sophie said.

"We stick together," he interrupted. "Okay?"

"Yeah, okay."

As they drove down the coast, Sophie gazed out at the sea. When the road took them inland for a while, she turned to Jack. His profile was just as interesting as the scenery and much more dear, at least to her.

"So you became a cop because of what happened with Lisa?" she ventured.

"Yeah," he said, sparing her a glance.

"Why did you quit?"

"Oddly enough, because of Lisa. Her unsolved murder got me into law enforcement, but the way every case seemed to echo hers drove me out of it."

"And here you are again," Sophie said.

"Yes, here I am again, but damn, this feels different. This isn't just a case of bad memories. This is déjà vu. I'd never forgive myself if I let Sabrina and Buzz down, but it's a slippery slope. On the one hand, I can't assume that just because there are similarities that it's the same kind of case. On the other hand, I can't assume because I'm sensitive to overreacting that I'm misreading things. So in the end, I have to trust what my eyes see and what my gut tells me."

"And it tells you to go back to the hotel?"

"And show the composite sketch around. I should have gotten a picture of Louis Nash to show around, too. Damn, why didn't I think of that?"

"I'll look on the internet and see if he has one."

She did just that while the miles sped by but in the end had to admit defeat. "Lots of pictures attributed to him but none of him."

"Is he a good photographer?"

Sophie looked at a couple of examples of his work. "Not bad. Some of the girls look a little…provocative, but that may just be the way they wanted to look."

As they drove into the hotel parking lot a few minutes later, Jack threw her a grin. "Well, here we are again." He found a parking spot up close to the front doors.

"I wonder if Paul Rey followed us," she asked. "For that matter, I wonder if he followed us out to the search area up in Astoria, too? What's he making of all this?"

"Who knows, but I have a feeling he's around here somewhere. I tried watching for a tail but this guy is apparently pretty good at disappearing and until we know what he's driving—"

"You'd think his mother and brother would have called him off by now and told him the gig is up."

"I don't think he's communicating with anyone," Jack said, holding the front door open for her. "He might be obsessive, his head set on one goal—kill Sabrina, then hit his brother up for half of what you get once she's dead. His family refers to him as a loose cannon. Maybe he's crazy enough to work in a void of his own making."

They bypassed the front desk and went downstairs, where the hubbub of the conference was over. Tuesday at noon seemed quiet at the hotel, perfect for Jack's intention of showing the sketch around.

Finding someone to show it to seemed to be the issue, however. Many of the people they'd grown accustomed to seeing were at home as the hotel had cut back hours once the rush was over. Still, they persevered, starting down in the kitchen and housekeeping, working their way up as they tried to find Jerry or Brad or Adam.

They finally found a guy painting the trim around a large window at the end of a hall on the third floor. As if sensing their interest in him, he paused in his task and looked over his shoulder as they approached. For some reason, his measuring gaze made Sophie extremely uncomfortable.

He was a tall, thin man with intense black eyes and longish black hair.

"Are you Adam?" Jack asked.

The guy kept his paintbrush poised on the wall as he leveled a steely stare at Jack. "I'm Adam."

"You're sure handy with that paintbrush," Jack said.

"What can I do for you? It's just me here right now. Give me your room number or better yet, call the front desk and get on the list. It may be morning before someone gets to you, though."

Jack showed him the composite sketch captured on his phone.

Adam stared at it and as he did so, Sophie looked from the sketch to the man gazing at it and almost fell over. They looked so much alike it was uncanny.

"Who is this?" he asked.

Sophie spoke up. "A man we need to ask a few questions," she said.

"Does he limp by any chance?"

They hadn't mentioned the limp, keeping that back in case someone recognized the sketch. Sophie could sense Jack fighting to rein in his excitement. "Yeah. He limps."

"I saw him Saturday. Up here, as a matter of fact. He was wheeling a cart with a couple of suitcases and a trunk on it."

"How big was the trunk?" Jack asked and Sophie could hear the edge in his voice.

Adam held out his arms. "Sizable."

"Did you see him unload the baggage or have any

idea to whom it belonged or by chance see what he was driving?"

Adam shook his head. "I saw him for about thirty seconds on my way to snake a plugged toilet. I didn't see no tags or nothing else. He was just pushing the cart into the service elevator and then he was gone and I was off."

"I'm calling Reece," Jack told Sophie.

"Ask him to get a picture of Louis Nash."

"I will."

As Jack took a few steps to use his phone in privacy, Adam asked why they wanted to know about the guy.

"A woman who looks a lot like me went missing from this hotel last Saturday," she said. "Police will want to question this man if we can find him. They'll probably want to ask you some questions, as well."

"Me?"

"About what you saw."

He shook his head. "Well, they have until five, 'cause that's when I'm leaving here. I have a lot to do on my new place."

"Is it here in town?"

He narrowed his eyes. "No. Why do you ask?"

She shrugged. "Well, you know, if the police want to talk to you—"

"I can talk to 'em here as well as there. Anyway, it's getting late. You got nothing else you want from me, I need to finish this job."

"Sure, only did you know Hank Tyson, the maintenance man who was killed last weekend?"

"Not really," he said. "Brad knows him. Knew him."

"How do you know Brad?"

"We worked together in Idaho a few years back. What's with all the questions?"

Jack's return saved her a response. "Reece is calling Sergeant Jones down here in Seaport," he said. "Time for us to get back to Astoria."

As they hurried back to the car, Jack added, "Reece said he went over to Nash's house after we left. He said the guy was totally cooperative. He remembered taking the photo of Sabrina, thought it was one of his better efforts. Reece also said Nash has an alibi for the weekend but that he invited Reece to search his house claiming he has nothing to hide."

"Did Reece conduct a search?"

"No. It's easy to tell he thinks we're barking up the wrong tree."

"Maybe we are," Sophie said. "Didn't you notice Adam Cook looks like the sketch?"

"I did notice that but he doesn't limp."

"You were never sure the limp was real, remember? You said it could have been a temporary injury or even a faked diversion. Notice how quick Adam was to point out that the man he said he saw had a limp. Did he do that to avert suspicion from himself?"

"Sophie, I don't know. If that guy took Sabrina would he be painting window trim three days later?"

"I don't know—you're the expert. But I have to remind you of one thing. We're not looking for Lisa's murderer, we're looking for the guy who abducted Sabrina, and in that mind-set, a limp doesn't matter."

"Neither does looking like a guy in a ten-year-old sketch," Jack said.

She sighed. "It seems almost impossible without the police reviewing surveillance tapes and questioning people more stringently. But can we afford not to consider everything and everyone? Remember when we talked to Brad Sunday morning? He said that Adam left here to go get a part. If he'd already stuffed Sabrina into a trunk and rolled her downstairs into a van, what better time to get her away from the hotel and Brad's prying eyes than to fake an errand? Or maybe he had Hank in the van, too. Maybe that's when he dumped the poor man's body."

"A hardware store would have a record of a sale. And damn it all, someone needs to check the hotel's security cameras."

"Oh, and, Jack, Adam said he was leaving town after work to go work on his new house. He was defensive and nervous and he looked at me like—I don't know, he just gave me the creeps."

THEY DROVE BY the Cromwell house and were reassured when Jack recognized an unmarked police car parked down the street. A second later, a taxicab drove by. Was that Sabrina returning from wherever the hell she'd been? The cab kept going and once again disappointment took a giant bite out of Jack's gut.

And that right there was the trouble with this whole thing. He might criticize Reece for not damning the torpedoes and investigating Sabrina's disappearance as a criminal act and yet he himself could go from thinking she'd been carted off in a trunk to holding his breath that she might miraculously emerge from a taxicab.

Jack had a sudden whim. "There's somewhere I want to go before we settle in to search the house again. Mind coming with me?"

"Are you kidding? There's nowhere I'd rather be than with you."

He grinned at her. "The feeling is mutual."

"So, where to now?"

He glanced over at her again, inordinately glad she wanted to be with him and very aware of how patient she was. They'd had coffee for breakfast, and a drive-through chicken sandwich for lunch. Not much of a romantic day after their first sexual encounter. She deserved dozens of red roses and champagne and boxes of chocolates—he wanted to shower her with attention. He wanted to be the man who erased the despicable Danny from her memory forever and showed her what a relationship could be like with someone who loved her.

Because he did love her. A half dozen times that day he'd wanted to tell her so. That morning when they awoke and she smiled up at him and kissed his lips. Later, in the shower, then when she reassured Sue—such a kind thing to do. And during all this, he knew her insides were twisted into a terrible knot as she worried about her sister. She was growing more vibrant by the day, an unselfish and generous woman with a huge heart. He loved her.

He lifted her hand from her lap. "Sophie, I have to tell you something."

"Uh-oh," she said. "That sounds ominous."

"No, it's nothing bad, at least I don't think so. I just want to tell you that I'm aware we've known each other a lot less time than you knew Danny and you thought he moved too fast, but I know how I feel—"

"Shh," she said softly. "Don't say anything. I feel the same way about you, like I want to announce to the world that you're it, that you're the only one for me. But we've known each other just a handful of days and they haven't been typical days for either of us." She laughed softly. "The horrible truth, my darling, is that I am the most boring woman you are ever going to meet. After this is over, you'll see I'll put you to sleep every time I open my mouth. You'll want to run for the hills."

"Oh, Sophie, that's not true and I think you know it."

"This is true. I don't even know if you like oatmeal or walks on the beach or what kind of movies—"

"Who cares about that stuff? Those are the things people find out about each other over time."

"Well, then, how about the fact that you live six hours south of me?"

"More like nine. I'll move, you'll move, we'll work it out. That's what people who care about each other do."

"And then there's Sabrina and Buzz and the immediate future and the potential wreckage—it's too much to think about right now. Let's just be in the moment, okay? Tell me where we're going."

"I just hope by the time you're ready to hear me

out, I haven't forgotten what I was going to say," he teased her.

She punched him in the side and laughed.

"We're going to Louis Nash's house. I looked it up on the internet. It's not far from here."

"What do you hope to find out?"

"I just want to get a feel for the guy, see where he lives, what he's like."

They found Nash's residence on a steep street two blocks off the main avenue. Jack parked a couple of doors down and they both spent five minutes sitting in the car watching to see if anyone else parked nearby or drove by suspiciously. They both had an image of Paul Rey in their head now and that should help if Paul got close to Sophie again.

"I have a gun in the trunk," he said.

"Why is it in the trunk?"

"It's back there with the handcuffs, a rifle, the stun gun—all the usual accruements. But I'm not a cop, I'm a private citizen, especially up here in Oregon where my license doesn't even mean as much as it does in California. The stakes go way up when you introduce a lethal weapon. If you carry it, you'd better be prepared to use deadly force. All that said, I'm going to go get it out of the trunk and you're going to use it if Paul Rey approaches this car. Okay?"

"I've never shot a gun."

"I'll show you how." He retrieved the gun, once again scanning the peaceful street that had no new cars parked on it and no pedestrians lingering on the sidewalks. He got back in the car and quickly acquainted her with the weapon. "It's all set to shoot. Just take off the safety, aim and pull the trigger. Got it?"

"I got it. But I don't want to kill Paul. He might know something about Sabrina."

"If he's walking up to this car he's got one thing on his mind, honey, and it isn't a chat. Protect yourself. Promise me."

"Okay, yeah, I will. I promise."

He leaned across the seat and touched her lips with his. "Are you as scared as you look?" he whispered.

"Yes, but mostly because I don't want to shoot anyone."

"I'll be back in ten minutes."

"Make it nine."

"You got it." He kissed her again, then walked quickly down the street toward Nash's house.

A small sign on the door read: Nash Photography. Please Knock. He knocked.

The door was answered by a tall, dark man in his midforties. Longish dark hair framed a lean, almost gaunt face dominated by large, heavily lidded eyes.

"Are you Louis Nash?" Jack asked pleasantly, but the truth was the dude raised his hackles on sight. Did he look like the sketch of Lisa's killer? About as much as Adam Cook did. The fact was that Jack had seen dozens of tall, drawn-looking guys over the years who resembled the sketch. This man had more angles in his face, was certainly older. There were surface similarities, but having never actually seen Lisa's killer in the flesh, he couldn't go so far as to say this was the guy.

And there was that conundrum again, that concern

that his subconscious was hell-bent on merging Lisa's killer and Sabrina's abductor no matter how unlikely the possibility.

"I heard you were the best photographer in town," Jack said, deciding on the spot not to mention Sabrina.

"One of them, yeah."

"My fiancée and I are getting married this summer. I was hoping you could show me some of your work."

Jack sensed Louis's reluctance. It could mean he had something to hide or he could just be in the middle of something. Maybe the detective's visit earlier that day had put him on his guard. Or here was a thought: maybe he sensed that Jack wasn't being honest.

"I have a few minutes," he said at last. "Come on in."

Jack stepped inside. A steep flight of stairs led upward to his left. The house was messy and cluttered, the walls covered with blown-up photos of kids and trees and oceanscapes.

"Have a seat at the table," Louis said as he swept aside what looked like lunch dishes to make space. "I'll go get the book."

He limped out of sight into a room whose door he closed behind him. He limped—right leg. Could mean something, could mean nothing. Jack used the opportunity to check out what he could see of the house. A closed door off the kitchen could be a pantry. It could also be access to a basement. It took all his willpower not to dash up the stairs or open every closed door, but he could hear Nash's returning footsteps. There wasn't time. If he wanted to poke around, he'd have to get Louis out of the room again.

Nash showed up with two books, one small and one album size. "This is a wedding I did last summer," he said, handing Jack the album.

Jack set it on the table and opened it. "Thanks. How many years have you been taking pictures?"

"Most of my life," Louis said.

"You must really enjoy it."

"Yeah, I do."

"This close-up picture of the bride eating cake is really nice."

"Thanks. Standard photo op."

"I was just thinking it must be hard photographing outdoor events around unpredictable Oregon coast weather. It would have to be easier in someplace more reliable. Like Southern California, for instance, where it's sunny most of the time."

"I suppose."

"Ever been down there?"

"In California?"

Jack flashed a smile. "Yeah."

Louis Nash's expression turned into a scowl. "Maybe. What's it to you?"

Jack shrugged. It was impossible not to notice that Louis had gone from cautious to angry. "Just curious—"

"Damn it all. Marie sent you, didn't she!"

"Marie?" Jack didn't have to pretend to be thrown off balance. "Who's Marie?"

"Are you another one of her private dicks?"

"I don't know—"

"'Cause, yeah, I know I'm in arrears with alimony. This business barely supports me. I have a mother, too, you know, and she needs stuff—Marie has a great job. For eleven years that woman has been making my life a living hell. I'm going to get a lawyer and put an end to this. You tell her that!"

Jack shook his head. "I don't know anyone named Marie. I'm not here for anything like that. I just need a photographer this summer, that's all."

Louis's balled fists relaxed a little. "She didn't send you?"

"No."

"Oh, man," Louis said, rubbing his face. "Sorry."

"It's okay. Exes can drive a man nuts."

"Ain't that the truth?"

Was Nash a sociopathic killer or a man hounded by an ex-wife? A list of questions to be answered built in Jack's head. "These pictures are of a beach wedding. My girl is traditional. She wants a church. Do you have photos of a wedding like that?"

Louis took a calming breath. "I'm doing one tomorrow morning right down the street. Come back on the weekend and you can see the pictures."

"How about tomorrow night?"

"They won't be ready. Besides, I'm closed tomorrow night."

"Don't you have other church weddings you could show me?"

"As a matter of fact," Nash said as he snapped the appointment book shut. "It doesn't much matter. I'm booked every weekend in July. Afraid I can't help you."

"Maybe we could reschedule—"

"I'm booked clear through the summer," Nash interrupted. They stared at each other again. A noise coming from outside caught both their attention. Jack scrambled to his feet and took off for the front door. He knew the sound of a gunshot when he heard one. He tore the door open and exited onto the wooden porch in time to see a green taxicab with a black diamond on the door pull away from the curb. His heart almost stopped in his chest as he took in the rest of the scene.

The passenger door of his car was open and Sophie lay on the sidewalk clutching some kind of colorful paper in her right hand. Blood soaked her left sleeve. His feet pounded the cement as he ran to kneel beside her.

She was almost as ashen as the cement on which she lay, eyes glassy. His heart started beating again when a dark tendril of hair fluttered against her cheek with an exhaled breath.

She looked up at him as though trying to place him, her gaze traveling between him and Nash, who had followed Jack outside at a slower pace and now stood looking over Jack's shoulder.

"Call an ambulance," Jack said, his voice cracking. Louis turned on his heels and limped back to his house.

How many victims had he knelt over in his life? Dozens. And not one of them had caused this blind panic building in his gut. "Sweetheart," he said softly as he lifted her right hand and pried her fingers from a stranglehold on what he now saw was a city map. "Sophie?"

"I don't need an ambulance," she finally mumbled.

"The hell you don't," Jack said, hoping Louis had

phoned for help. He dug in his pocket for his phone. "Hang in there, honey."

"I…I," she whispered as she gazed up at his eyes.

He squeezed her hand. "Don't worry, everything will be—"

"I didn't recognize him."

Jack paused from entering the emergency number just in case Louis hadn't. "Paul Rey?"

"He had a beard…"

"Shh," he said. "Stay still."

"A taxi… Oh, Jack, I…hurt."

"I know, baby," he said, stroking her hair away from her face. She'd hit her forehead when she fell and now blood trickled toward her eyes. He found a bandanna in his pocket and dabbed at it as he studied her. Had there ever been a moment in his life when he hadn't known every single detail of her gently arched eyebrows, that lovely little mole on her cheek, the shape of her lips? He knew there had been but it seemed a lifetime ago.

"I hear a siren," he said when the high-pitched wail registered in his brain. He looked back toward Nash's house but the front door was firmly shut. "Here's the ambulance. Try to be still."

The emergency crew swarmed around her and Jack stepped away. While they stabilized her, he deposited the map into the empty paper bag from their lunch stop so he could give it to the police. He couldn't imagine Rey would have finally left prints but procedures were procedures. He looked for his gun, hoping Danny's brother hadn't taken it—wouldn't a stolen firearm be a fun thing to explain to Reece? But he quickly found it in the center console, where Sophie must have slipped it out of sight.

He answered the ambulance driver's questions and watched as they loaded Sophie into the narrow ambulance. Before he got in his car to follow her to the hospital, he called Detective Reece and reported what had happened.

"That damn fool," Reece groaned. "Why can't we catch him? I'll get a crew out to the scene to gather evidence and meet you at the hospital. If they keep her there overnight, we'll protect her room."

"You and me both," Jack responded.

Chapter Eleven

"How do you feel?" Jack asked her several hours later.

Sophie had been sedated through the process of cleansing, stitching and bandaging her arm and had awoken to hear the doctor tell her that she was going to spend the night for observation. Ensconced in a room she had all to herself, she watched as a woman wearing a pink smock covered with frolicking kittens came through the door wheeling a blood pressure machine.

"Hi, my name is Joy," the woman said, addressing Sophie. "I'll be your nurse until midnight. Right now I need to get your vitals and things."

Detective Reece started to leave the room.

"You don't have to go yet," Joy said. She reminded Sophie of a cupcake: round, smiling, rosy cheeked, dark brown curls bunched on top of her head like a dollop of chocolate frosting. "I can work around you."

"So how do you feel?" Jack repeated.

How Sophie felt was shot up, washed out and sleepy. "I feel stupid," she said because that's what she felt the most of.

"So Paul Rey was wearing some sort of disguise?"

"He had a beard and his eyes were dark instead of blue. He didn't look anything at all like Danny's brother." With that comment, she included a glance at Detective Reece, who stood at the foot of her bed. "Nothing like the picture you showed us."

"What exactly happened?" Reece asked.

Sophie took a steadying breath. Joy had finished with the blood pressure and now stood by with a thermometer poised for insertion in her mouth. "I was sitting there with Jack's gun in my hand ready to shoot Paul Rey if he dared show up. Then this cab pulled to the curb in front of the car. The driver got out, smiled at me and waved a map. His body language said he was lost and needed help. I put Jack's gun in the glove compartment so he wouldn't see it and I got out of the car to help the guy." She looked from one man to the other and added, "Let me reemphasize that he didn't look anything like Danny's brother."

"Then what?"

"He spread the map out on the hood of Jack's car and I leaned over to look at it. The next thing I knew, I detected movement out of the corner of my eye and in that moment, I knew what a fool I'd been, that he was Paul Rey and he had a gun. I turned toward him and grabbed it."

"The gun?" Reece asked, eyebrows raised.

"Yes. I grabbed it and he fired. For a second I didn't understand why my left arm went numb when I'd grabbed the muzzle with my right hand and then I realized the bullet had entered that arm. I looked in his eyes before I guess I fainted. The next thing I knew, Jack was kneeling by my side and Paul was gone."

"Good heavens," Reece said, his cherubic face now wearing a stunned expression. "You are one very lucky young woman. I have a CSI team out there right now. They'll find the bullet... We can match it to the one he fired over at the Cromwell house."

"If you ever catch him, you'll have a good case," Jack said not without irony. "Were there any results from the other foot searches this afternoon?"

"Not a thing," Reece said.

Jack gently touched Sophie's shoulder and she rested her cheek against his warm hand. The nurse took the opportunity to stick the thermometer in her mouth.

Reece continued. "Thanks to your description of the taxi we were able to narrow it down to Green Diamond Cabs. They're a small enterprise that operates a grand total of four units. They figure one of the cars was stolen off their unmonitored lot last night. They hadn't even missed it yet. We found it abandoned out near a rock quarry."

"We drove by Buzz's house when we got back after talking to Adam Cook down in Seaport," Jack said. "Rey must have picked us up there."

As Joy withdrew the thermometer and started entering data into a computer affixed to the wall, Sophie spoke. "We saw a green cab, remember?"

"That's right," Jack said. "Damn. I should have stayed away from the Cromwell house. I figured even Rey wouldn't show up with an unmarked car out front."

"He's either a lot smarter than we think he is or a lot luckier than he has a right to be," Reece said.

"What did you think of Adam Cook's story?" Jack asked Reece. "For that matter, what have you found out about the man himself? And what about getting the hotel's surveillance tapes?"

"Gentlemen," Joy said. "Perhaps you would be so kind as to continue your conversation in the hall while I ask Ms. Sparrow a few questions?"

Jack raised Sophie's hand to his lips and kissed her knuckles. "I'll be right back," he said.

"And I'm posting a guard on your door," Reece added as both men exited the room.

Sophie answered a dozen questions about her health in general and her pain level in particular. Despite Jack's protective streak and Reece's assurances of a guard at her door, she had no desire to be drugged out on pain meds so she said she felt fine. Still, she'd been given something for the procedure where they worked on her arm and the truth was she was having trouble keeping her eyes open.

"I couldn't help overhearing you talking to the detective," Joy said.

"Oh. Well, everyone is trying to catch the nutcase who shot me."

"Of course. My husband is a firefighter and two of his best friends are with the sheriff's office. I know all about shop talk and questions, Lordy, do I."

"I bet you do. Does your husband work here in Astoria?"

"Yep. See, that's what I overheard. You talked about

the Cromwell house and I know Buzz is in Antarctica and Charlie, that's my husband, said something about searching for Sabrina… Is she okay, do you know? I keep waiting to hear something on the news…" She narrowed her eyes and gave Sophie a closer look. "I didn't notice this before what with the bandage on your forehead and you lying down and all. You bear a striking resemblance to Sabrina Cromwell, don't you?"

"I'm her twin sister," Sophie said and managed not to burst into tears.

"I didn't even know she had a twin."

"It's a long story," Sophie said.

"Oh, gosh, when Charlie mentioned an informal search, my heart just about dropped. I hope she's okay. She's the nicest person. Charlie was away at training when my last baby came early— it was Sabrina who came over to the house to drive me to the hospital and watch my three-year-old until my mother could get here. And we're not even close friends. And what she did for Charlie's buddy and coworker, well, it was great. If she hadn't gone out of her way to talk to him… Anyway, I saw his wife last week and she was smiling for the first time in weeks and gushed about a trip… Well, Sabrina is a doll."

Sophie just stared at the woman. Something she'd just said rang a distant bell but the words had begun to all run together. She fought to stay awake but it was a losing battle.

Sometime later she opened her eyes to find Jack asleep in a chair at the foot of her bed. "Jack?" she whispered and he instantly opened his eyes and joined her.

His kiss was sensual but brief. "This isn't how I planned on spending our second night together," he said.

"Me neither."

"How are you feeling?"

"Chilled. Is it cold in here?"

"Not really," he said, and kissed her forehead. "You feel warm to me," he added as he laid the back of his fingers against her cheek.

"Never mind that. Jack, I need to call my mother and let her know I was hurt but that I'm okay."

"Your mother," he said as if surprised.

"Yes. My mother. I don't want to shut her out of my life and that includes the bad things, too."

"I'll get your phone. It's in your purse—"

"No, that's okay, it's too late to call her tonight. I'll wait till morning." She blinked her eyes a couple of times.

Jack felt her forehead again. "I'm calling the nurse," he said but before he could press the call button, the curtain parted and Joy walked in. "Last vitals for my shift," she chirped.

"I was just about to call you," Jack said. "Sophie feels warm."

Joy produced a thermometer. A moment later she read the results. "It's not too bad but I'll get the doctor on call, just to be on the safe side. Don't worry, this isn't uncommon."

Sophie endured an exam that ruled out all serious causes and was started on an antibiotic to be on the safe side. By the time things had settled down, Joy had left for the night and Jack looked as tired as she was.

"Why don't you go back to Buzz's house and get some sleep," she said as he pulled a chair up to the head of her bed.

"I don't want to leave you."

"I know, but I just need sleep. There's a guard on the door."

"But—"

"Sabrina is still missing," Sophie reminded him.

"I know that."

"It's past midnight. Buzz will be home today, right?"

"Tonight, yeah, I see what you're saying. Okay, I'll continue the search." He stared down into her eyes as he added, "Whether you're ready to hear it or not, the fact is, I love you, Sophia Sparrow."

She smiled into his eyes. She'd never said those three words to anyone but assorted pets, stuffed animals and her parents but she whispered them now without hesitation. "I love you, too, Jack Travers."

He kissed her again and she closed her eyes as he left the room.

WIDE AWAKE AFTER the drive back to the Cromwell house, Jack spent an hour searching Sabrina's office for anything to do with Kyle or anyone else for that matter. He checked the emails on her computer—nothing abnormal. She communicated with Kyle and Sue and Buzz and dozens of other people, including the woman Sophie had mentioned, Bunny. He read through everything that was recent but there was nothing to suggest any clandestine romance or that she'd so much as entertained the idea of running off to meet anyone let alone actually done it. It didn't surprise him that a thorough search didn't reveal any indication Sabrina had returned to the house after talking to Jack.

The conversation he'd had that evening at the hospital with Reece hadn't been very productive. While Reece was apologetic about his department's inability to find Paul Rey, they were still dragging their feet on Louis Nash. He learned that Reece wasn't aware Louis had an ex-wife but then he'd laughed and said, "Who doesn't?"

As for Adam Cook, Jack learned he currently lived in Brad Withers's basement in a relatively small house. Where did he get the money to buy a new place? While it was true he had a criminal record in another state, his nose had been clean for several years. The Seaport police promised to look into him more closely in the days to come and Reece assured Jack that the police had requested and tomorrow would review the hotel's security tapes.

And meanwhile, time ticked away.

Jack felt like throwing something across the room. How was it possible Sophie had been shot by that bozo Paul Rey when every law enforcement type in the county was looking for him? How was it possible Sabrina had been missing for days without anyone but him and Sophie and her friends at the firehouse taking it seriously? How was it going to be possible to face Buzz tonight without any news about his cherished wife?

He poured himself a finger of his friend's whiskey and sat in a chair in front of the unlit fireplace. He had far less than twenty-four hours. The mantel clock struck three. He set the booze aside and went to bed.

He awoke the next morning to a phone call and answered it as he rubbed the sleep out of his eyes.

"Hey, lover boy, you sound like someone who slept in." Hearing Sophie's voice was the best way to wake up. Well, second best.

"Who me? I've been up for hours," he said with a laugh. "Do you miss me?"

"Like crazy. But you're never going to believe who's coming to visit me today."

"Don't tell me it's Danny Privet."

"Funny you should mention *his* name. I called him this morning to tell him to call off his sicko brother."

"And what did he say?"

"He said his lawyer told him not to talk to me. He also said even if he knew how, he wouldn't."

"Wow. I'm guessing it's not Danny coming to visit you."

"It's my mother. She's getting a lady from her church to drive her over after lunch."

"Will you still be in the hospital?" Jack asked.

"Yeah, afraid so. The fever came back. They're being cautious because I don't live locally. Did you find anything in Sabrina's house?"

"Nothing."

"I keep thinking I'm missing something," Sophie said. "Like what?"

"I don't know. I need to talk to Joy. She comes on at noon."

"Joy?"

"The nurse. I think she said something yesterday that I was too groggy to pick up on. All we need is something to convince the police that Sabrina isn't off on her own free will, right?"

"Or under Paul Rey's control. They still think he might be responsible for everything. It doesn't seem to matter how many times I try to explain about him confusing her for you. I think they're so focused on catching him that nothing else matters."

"You'll work this out, honey," Sophie said. "I know you will."

He hoped she was right. "I'll be at the hospital after I do a few things like talk to Adam Cook and search Louis Nash's place."

"Sounds like fun. Be careful."

Jack's first priority was to talk to Adam Cook but the man didn't answer his phone. He recalled Sophie's telling him Adam had said he was going to work on a house. Vowing not to involve Reece or any other cop unless necessary, he tried looking up Brad Withers's telephone number.

"Yeah, Adam can be hard to get ahold of when he goes up to Glenville to work on his house. Some cousin left him the place but it was a real wreck. He's desperate to get out of my basement, though, so he works on it every chance he gets. He claims he doesn't get good cell service because of all the forest around the place.

You said it's important you talk to him so I'll give you his address but don't expect a real warm welcome."

"I'm not sure where Glenville is," Jack said. So that's how the man had gotten a new house—he'd inherited it.

"It's a few miles southeast of Astoria. There's nothing but a sign on Highway 101. Adam's new place is off the road, 33401 Madrone. Real remote."

How handy for illegal activity, Jack thought but all he said was, "Thanks."

He drove by three churches before he saw one being readied for a wedding. Dashing inside, he found a florist setting a single spray by the altar, and created a story about being the bride's brother and asking if the woman knew what time the wedding started.

"In fifteen minutes. Where is everybody?"

"I'm not sure," Jack said.

"It's a crazy time for a wedding, isn't it? Who gets married at eleven thirty on a Wednesday morning? I mean even though it's a really small wedding…" The woman seemed to recall she was talking to a supposed member of the family and smiled. "Of course, love does as love wants."

"Right," he said. "I'll just go outside and wait."

He drove off instead, finding Nash's van—obvious because of the photography sign on its side—parked in the alley behind the man's house. He found a spot at the throat of the alley where he could see when the van left. He'd tucked his revolver into his shoulder holster before leaving the house that morning and checked now to make sure it was invisible. What he'd told Sophie was true. A gun could escalate a confrontation into a life-or-death battle. On the other hand, he didn't know what was inside Nash's house—or who. If Louis had nabbed Sabrina, then the stakes were already through the roof.

At last, Nash limped with purpose to the van carrying a bag of equipment and a tripod. He threw his gear into the back of the van and roared off. Jack left his car where he'd parked it and approached the back of Nash's house on foot. Pausing at the door, he looked for the telltale signs of an alarm system and saw nothing, but that didn't mean there wasn't one. Throwing caution to the wind, he picked the lock and entered the house.

Profound silence greeted his entry into the kitchen that was cluttered with unwashed dishes and bags and boxes of food. As he locked the outside door, he got his bearings. The door he'd noticed the afternoon before turned out to be unlocked and that came as a disappointment. If he was going to hide someone, he'd sure as heck lock the door. The landing behind the door was actually a small pantry with a few shelves covered with what looked like surplus food items. He walked past those until he came across a flight of stairs. He flicked a light to illuminate them and descended with his heart beating overtime.

What he found was an elaborate studio. Photos Nash must have taken himself hung on the walls. Curtained-off areas looked like changing rooms while hooks held different robes and hats maybe for use as props or costumes. A small stage with adjustable lighting took up a corner while an assortment of chairs lined yet another wall.

He lifted area rugs looking for hidden spaces, tapped walls and peeked under paintings and curtains all to no avail. This was obviously the public face of Nash's business and a dead end for Jack.

He immediately made his way to the living room and went up the stairs. He did a quick search of each room, behind mirrors, under drawers, searching for a trunk or some clue the guy had been down in Seaport a couple of days before. Satisfied there was nothing to find, he went back downstairs and picked the lock on the room Nash had disappeared into the day before. It turned out to be a small office. The closet was secured with a serious lock. Ignoring that for the moment, he zeroed in on a locked file cabinet. He found the keys to that in the desk drawer under the felt liner.

It looked like business as usual to him as he thumbed through the files without much enthusiasm until he saw a folder labeled Cases. The file contained several head shots of women including the one of Sabrina. Each had a number on them between one and three. He took a photo of everything. Another file labeled Betty Nash/ Mother drew his attention. It contained a mass of forms and old insurance papers along with a recently issued uncashed social security check made out to Betty Nash. He quickly scanned a stapled compilation of her recent bank statements and the deed to a house in her name located on 40105 Manzanita Drive. Maybe the woman would have insights into her son. He needed a map of the area both to locate this house and to find Adam Cook's new property.

He continued taking photos of anything that looked pertinent. Over an hour had gone by since he entered the house. Wedding photos could take forever, but he didn't have forever to spend. It was well after noon now. Buzz's plane landed in Portland at 7:05 this evening. Give him three hours to claim his luggage, rent a car and drive here. That meant he'd be back by ten and that meant that by then, Jack either had to be sitting beside Sabrina on her sofa or know exactly where she was and why.

Was he spinning his wheels, trying so hard to stay busy that it was all for show? For all he knew, Louis Nash had abducted Sabrina days ago, killed her and disposed of her body. He could be looking for a ghost.

A steely reserve flooded his body. Buzz needed to come home to facts, not haunting maybes. Sophie, if denied her sister, had to at least have the truth of her death. No one could move forward without understanding the past, so in that way, whether Sabrina was alive or not did nothing to negate the importance of finding her.

He heard a sound at the back door and froze. Footsteps echoed in the old house. Jack quietly closed the file drawer and locked it again. He replaced the cabinet key. A closet beckoned to him from across the room but there wasn't time to get there—he took the only option he could see: he dived under the desk but it didn't have a solid back and if Nash happened to look at the desk from the right angle, there was going to be an issue.

A second later he heard a key in the door and that's when he recalled he hadn't locked it after himself. There was a pause and then the door opened. Jack's view was of six inches of brown trouser leg and two worn-looking loafers that didn't move as Nash must have surveyed the room for signs of an intruder. Jack made himself as small as possible, holding his breath. At last, Nash moved—perhaps he decided he must have forgotten to lock the door before leaving the house. Another key in another lock and the closet door swung open. Nash rifled through the contents, grunting when he apparently found what he wanted. He finally limped to the desk and dropped a gray duffel bag with black straps on the floor. It hit with a metallic clang. Jack drew in his legs as Nash sat down and swiveled the chair toward the file cabinet.

What was in that bag? Tripods, maybe? Lighting trees? And what was Nash doing back here so soon anyway?

Nash apparently retrieved the key from the desk drawer, then opened the file cabinet. The drawer rolled out, papers rustled, the drawer slammed shut and, once again, Jack heard the sound of a key in a lock. Nash got to his feet, hefted the bag with a grunt and walked out of the office.

Jack stayed where he was until he heard the outside door slam shut. Curious about what Nash had taken from the file cabinet, he immediately searched the desk drawer, but the key was no longer under the felt.

The closet that had been locked before now stood open. Did that mean that whatever Nash took from here in a duffel bag was the only thing he safeguarded? Jack's quick perusal of the rest of the closet found nothing but photograpy equipment. He glanced at his watch. It was time to cut his losses and leave this house.

Once in his car he drove past the church. The lot was empty, which suggested the wedding party was gone. Maybe Nash dropped by his house to get something he needed for the reception photos.

Jack kept driving, unable to stop, knowing that time continued marching on like a determined soldier. He finally pulled to a stop in front of a small convenience store, where he made himself grab a premade sandwich because he'd skipped breakfast. As he ate the sandwich, he found Adam Cook's general location on the map on his phone and almost choked on salami and cheese.

Cook's new house and the town of Glenville were only a mile and a half from the search he and Sophie had participated in the day before. In fact, they'd driven by the road he lived on. What's more, Nash's mother's place was close to Cook's but separated by the river that had serenaded them as they looked for Sabrina. In other words, the search location, the Cook house and Nash's mother's place were all within a half mile of each other as the crow flies. Sophie's ominous statement came back to him: *I sense Sabrina is close by.*

And now his gut told him she'd been right.

With no bridge to cross the river, one had to go back out to the highway and travel north a quarter of a mile, turning onto a parallel road to travel east again, in effect making a giant U-turn. The three locations all but lined up on the GPS.

Jack immediately tossed the sandwich aside and headed out of town.

The skies were dark and foreboding. Driving through a part of town he wasn't familiar with, he made any number of wrong turns in his quest to find the main road. They all either emptied into other streets or dead-ended against the side of a mountain. Anxiety and frustration had him gripping the wheel so tight his knuckles turned white. Finally plugging the address into his phone's navigation, he followed the instructions, hoping he had enough service to get accurate directions. The synthesized voice actually calmed him and directed him south of town over the bridge crossing the Columbia River. A mile farther and it instructed him to turn east.

After ten more minutes of twists and hills, he turned onto Manzanita. As if exhausted by her diligent service his phone almost immediately lost service.

Living abodes this far out of the city were apparently built off on wandering driveways behind tall fences or acres of forest. The driveway leading to Betty Nash's place was overgrown with underbrush at first but soon cleared to what must be a beautiful meadow when the sun was out and the fields weren't muddy. Those fields held nothing now but a handful of wet cows.

The house itself was a stately looking gray two-story Victorian-influenced building. A dozen or more barns and outbuildings had sprung up around it over the years. Between the outbuildings and the tangle of old roads crisscrossing the land, he thought the place must have been a dairy farm once upon a time. Everything looked old, dejected and worn-out. He parked near the house and stepped onto a porch in serious need of repair. A knock on the door and a ring of the bell produced no results.

He tried yelling.

Nothing. Hadn't Reece said the woman was house-bound? If that were the case, she might very well be inside. Maybe she hadn't heard his knock. He tried the knob, his intention to open it a crack and call her name, but it was locked.

He stepped off the porch and walked to a nearby open building that looked as if it might be the garage. All it held was an old sedan circa 1960 up on blocks.

So, she might be inside, too disabled to answer the door. She might have had a friend give her a ride to an appointment. Hell, she might be looking out a win-dow right now holding a shotgun, deciding she wasn't about to open the door to a stranger—he didn't blame her if that was the case.

Did he try to search all the buildings? Several were out in the open, others abutted distant forests, and still others were nothing but dim shapes barely vis-ible through the misty skies. It would take hours.

Something was off about Nash, he just knew it. It all came back to proof and he had zip. If he wanted Betty Nash's insights into her son, he'd simply have to come back later with Reece.

He retraced his route, traveled south until he found Madrone and turned east again. It took a while, but he eventually ferreted out a sign nailed to a tree with the numbers 33401 painted in fading white paint. The drive was muddy from all the recent rain and very dark as the towering evergreens cut out the relative light in the sky. He expected to find a house under the process of renovation at the end of the drive, not the rickety-looking tan building that greeted him. If Adam was working here, it had to be on the interior.

There was no vehicle in sight or any sign that anyone was home. He knocked on the door and peeked through the window. The room he glimpsed was even darker than outside, sparsely furnished and very still. He wasn't surprised when no one responded to his knock or his voice calling out Adam's name.

A detached garage held a van. No trunks, no suitcases. Several big batteries stacked against a wall and, oddly enough, what appeared to be a new golf cart. Adam checked to make sure no one had appeared out of thin air before he opened the double back doors of the vehicle. He found a dozen boxes all sealed and randomly opened one of them to check the contents. It looked like the guy had visited a hardware store and stocked up on lantern fuel in case the electricity went out. Probably not an uncommon event out this far. There was no indication a dead handyman or an abducted woman had ever been in the van; indeed, as it now sat, there wasn't room for a human being back there.

Big fat raindrops started falling from the heavy clouds as he started a foot search of the land, following a fence as he moved while listening for the sound of an approaching engine. Just about convinced there was nothing to find, he ran across what appeared to be a worn path disappearing into the woods and followed it until it ended at a new building set out of sight from the house and sheltered by undergrowth.

The ruts in the path suggested Cook's shiny new golf cart had made this trip with a heavy cargo...

This building had to be where Cook was putting in his time. Overhead, he saw electricity lines connecting the building to the power pole and a spigot near the foundation promised water. Perhaps he was creating a whole other house back here. Jack walked around the entire structure. There were no windows. Odd. That precluded its use for human occupation. But it could be the shop. His father, a retired contractor, had often created a building similar to this one prior to construction. The single door was secured with a heavy chain and two different padlocks.

He studied the locks—no way could he pick them. If there was the slightest indication that Sabrina was being held here, he'd shoot the locks, but there just wasn't. In fact, face it, there was no indication at the Nash house or this one that anyone did anything wrong. Still, he pounded on the door and listened with his ear against the wood after calling Sabrina's name.

Striking out twice in a row and this late in the day was infuriating as well as heartbreaking. He headed back to town, determined to use what little time he had left to turn things around. Both Betty Nash's house and Adam's Cook place were well outside the city limits... He decided he'd stop and talk to the sheriff.

He drove back to Astoria with a bitter taste in his mouth.

AGAINST DOCTOR'S ORDERS, Sophie checked herself out of the hospital. The fever had been gone for hours and she was restless. While the visit with her mother had been stilted and thankfully short, it was one of the few times in Sophie's life where she could recall her mom trying hard to make a connection and she deeply appreciated the effort it took.

But what really drove her was the conversation with nurse Joy that had taken place after her mother's visit. She finally thought she could prove to Detective Reece that Sabrina had not run off with Kyle Woods.

As for Jack? He was hopefully doing what he knew how to do best and that was locating Sabrina, and there was no way she was going to get in the middle of that. She'd change places with her sister in a blink if she could, but the depressing fact was that there'd been no further sense of contact. Sabrina had disappeared, it seemed, from the earth and from Sophie's psyche.

She took a taxi—not a green one—back to the Cromwell house and used the back door key she'd taken from the hook in the kitchen the last time she was there. She was careful to relock the door before making her way to Sabrina's computer. The light was blinking on the desk answering machine and Sophie decided to listen to the messages. How ironic would it be if Sabrina had called home on the off chance someone was there to answer her call and no one knew it.

But the calls were from Jack, people at work, people Sophie didn't know, the vet's office and Buzz, all begging her to respond. And these were just the calls to the home phone—who knew how many had been made to Sabrina's cell wherever that was?

She'd heard them all and learned zilch. She pressed the save button, just in case...

Just in case this all wasn't as hopeless as it seemed. She switched on a lamp to combat the darkness, plugged in her cell to recharge the battery that had gone dead hours before and booted up the computer, where she looked for and found the email she recalled reading a couple of days ago.

Guess what? He asked me again. This time, I don't know, it was different. It was as though he was finally seeing me the way he used to... It made me remember what we once had. I know he's been confiding in you and I want you to know that your advice has been invaluable to both of us. I still love him and if we can make this marriage work, well, that would be wonderful. So, no calls, no email or texting, no internet or television. Just him and me in a friend's cabin, alone, together for five days. Maybe we can recapture what we lost.

Thanks for being his friend and mine. You're an angel. Have a great time on your hiking trip. Bunny.

On the night Sophie was shot, Joy had told her about her husband's friend with the broken marriage and the way Sabrina had helped. The friend's husband was a fireman just like Joy's husband was. Somewhere in her medicated mind, Sophie had connected some of these dots with this email she'd read days before, an email signed by Bunny, which today Joy confirmed was Barbara Woods's nickname.

Sabrina was Kyle's friend, not his lover. Kyle was off with Bunny in an apparently secluded location, purposely shutting out the world in a battle to win back his wife.

As Sophie picked up the desk phone to call Reece, the computer went dark and the lights went off, plunging the bedroom into near blackness. The sounds of the storm—the creaking, the rain pounding on the metal roof and the wind banging limbs against the windows—now escalated, making the unfamiliar house feel scary. She carefully found her way to the bedroom door from which, through the front window, she could see falling rain highlighted by the sidewalk lamps outside. A porch light flicked on down the block. And that upped the spook factor.

Hairs on the back of her neck rose for no reason. She had to get out of this house. She turned on her heels to run to the kitchen but an explosion of shattering glass drove her to the floor, where she instinctively covered her face. She heard a thud as something heavy landed inside the room with her, then crunching sounds. Glass pieces fell from her shoulders and hair as she scrambled to her feet. She glanced at what was left of the front window, where the dark hulking shape of a man approached through the rubble. She took off again, desperate to reach the back door, where she could escape into the neighbor's yard. She hadn't taken more than a half a dozen steps when two hands grabbed her from behind. A cloth covered her lower face, killing a scream before it could escape her throat. She sank into unconsciousness.

Chapter Twelve

It took a while to jump through the hoops but Jack finally found himself seated in Sheriff Leroy Donner's office. "You see, son, Reece," he said in what sounded like a Deep South drawl, "has to please Chief Holt and Holt has to please the commissioner—plus we're just getting over a holiday weekend. I swear, this whole city stops on a holiday, any holiday. Plus Reece is a cautious man. I am not. No siree. My calling card is blazing guns and everyone knows it."

Well, Jack had wanted someone who would act and it looked as though he'd found his man. Still, the guy was over the top. Big, florid, stuffed into his tan uniform and bursting with self-importance, he made a hard pill to swallow.

"I actually remember old Alastair Becket," Donner added. "He's the geezer who left Adam Cook that nice little piece of hillside up there near Glenville. Quiet guy. Traveled all over the countryside taking pictures and developing them in his basement darkroom. The library and courthouse are full of his work. Personally, I think it's boring."

Unlike, Jack supposed, the painting of a tiger hauling its prey off into the jungle that hung above the sheriff's desk. "There's a darkroom in the basement of that old house?" Jack asked.

"Yeah. Nice one, or at least it used to be."

He mentally slapped himself. Adam Cook had a link to photography, too. What if he'd also been taking pictures of Sabrina? Why hadn't Adam gone inside that dumpy tan house and looked for a basement?

"Anyway," the sheriff continued, "I wouldn't mind going up there and introducing myself to Adam, have a look around, push a few buttons. First thing tomorrow, that's what I'll do. If anything makes me suspect the guy is involved in Mrs. Cromwell's disappearance, I'll tear the place apart. You have my word."

"Your word is good enough for me," Jack said, and endured a bone-crushing handshake. He had hoped things would start happening tonight but maybe it was better this way. The sheriff was a bulldozer—pushing too hard in the wrong places might drive things forward with awful consequences.

One way or another, he'd finesse Cook into showing him the basement before the sheriff got there.

He left the station with big plans. First Cook's basement and, if that didn't produce any results, on to Betty Nash's place. If she'd been off to an appointment surely she'd be home by now. Back in the car, he checked his phone again and found that though he still hadn't received any calls, he had been sent a text from someone he didn't know two hours before.

Hi, it's me, Sophie, he read. I'm using Joy's phone

because my battery is dead. The thing is, I need to look at something at Sabrina's house so I'm taking a taxi over there (not with Paul Rey at the wheel, I promise). I don't want you to drop everything and come running, okay? Just wanted you to know that's where I am. I'll meet you there whenever. Love you.

His lips curved. She loved him.

He immediately punched in her number and once again, it went to voice mail. Must still be out of juice.

All the same, he decided to go to the Cromwell house before driving back out into the country to check Cook's and Nash's places. The car's wipers fought the deluge while an annoying bumper-hugging orange subcompact rode his tailpipe. He wasn't positive why he felt anxious unless he was worried Sophie might be in danger. Hell, as long as Paul Rey was running around loose, of course she was in danger! He took a wrong turn, twice, and gritted his teeth.

The sight of Buzz and Sabrina's utterly dark house on a block of illuminated homes took a big old bite out of his gut. He grabbed a flashlight out of the console and ran up the front walk to come to a dead halt on the porch. The front window was gone, broken, glass both inside and out. He glimpsed something at his feet and bent to pick up one of the hated origami foxes. He climbed into the living room, where glass covered almost every surface. He conducted a hasty search of the house and found Sophie's phone plugged in next to Sabrina's computer. The flashlight died as he searched the backyard. Dripping wet again, he called the police.

He gave Dispatch the address. "A woman has been

attacked and is now missing. Paul Rey may be chasing her. Get people out here to search the neighborhood. Her name is Sophia Sparrow. Have Reece call Jack Travers ASAP."

He ran outside and looked up and down the street, then he got in his car and unfolded his fist to reveal the crumpled dollar bill. Had they all underestimated Rey's determination and adaptability? He had been escalating his attempts—was this blatant in-your-face destruction his last step?

Jack's phone rang and his heart leaped but it was only Reece. "I've been trying to reach you," the detective said. "We finally heard from the fireman, Kyle Woods. He was off with his estranged wife. That leaves Sabrina Cromwell's safety an issue. The chief is finally willing to take this seriously."

"That's great," Jack said with all the patience he could muster. "But—"

"That's not all," Reece continued. "We got a call about fifteen minutes ago. Someone saw a man fitting Rey's description out by the state park. He's driving north in an older-model black Chevy with stolen plates. There was a dark-haired woman with him. My officers are keeping their distance while we work out the best way to go about stopping the car. There's no way of knowing if the woman is Sabrina—"

"Or Sophie," Jack interrupted. "She's been taken from the Cromwell house. I found her phone. I also found one of those origami foxes."

"That places Rey at the scene. Know when this all happened?"

"Not exactly but I called it in and I can hear sirens approaching. Your guys can question the neighbors. I'm on my way to join you," Jack said. He hung up as Reece told him to stay put. Sure.

He tore out of the subdivision right as two police cars rolled in. He kept going. It wasn't until he was a mile along that he noticed a car tagging him. Not again. He drove under a streetlight and glanced in his rear-view mirror in time to see an orange subcompact that looked just like the one that had followed him from the hospital to Sabrina's house.

The only person he knew who liked to follow people was Paul Rey. On the other hand, Paul Rey was, first, supposedly driving north in a stolen car, not southeast. Secondly, the man had proved pretty damned accomplished at remaining out of sight.

No rock unturned, he decided. Somewhere up here was one of those annoying unposted no-outlet streets that he'd run into earlier that day. He turned onto the first one that looked vaguely familiar. After a block or two, he realized this was the one that back-ended a forest preserve with a seasonal day park. He drove past the closed-for-the-season sign and hit a sawhorse barricade before circling the small parking lot, the orange car following. Then he immediately turned his bigger car to block the exit and got out. A man popped out of the orange compact, fired a round of shots that went wild and took off at a run down a heavily wooded path, his own headlights illuminating his retreating figure. Jack took off after him.

The helpful headlights extended until the path

curved and they were plunged into a dripping, dark world of massive ferns and towering trees. Jack chased the guy's shadowy silhouette and the hollow sound of his footsteps until the timbre of those steps changed. His quarry had to be on a bridge—wood by the sound of it. He heard a scrambling sound and an oath followed by a thud as his prey apparently lost footing and skated on mossy, slippery boards. There was the sound of a splash into the stream running under the bridge, then more oaths as Jack raced to get to the guy before he took off again. He reached for the writhing shape as it tried to slither from his grasp. With adrenaline pumping through his veins, he yanked the man to his feet.

He was too short to be Cook or Nash. Jack frisked him and found no weapon. "Where's your gun?" he demanded.

"I dropped it when I fell," the guy said. "Why are you chasing me?"

"Why am I chasing you?" Jack said. "Nice try." He marched his complaining catch back to the parking lot, where the headlights once again proved their worth.

The guy was covered in wet moss and slime. "Paul Rey," Jack said. "Why am I not surprised?"

"Reynard. My name is Paul Reynard."

"Your mother shortened the name two decades ago."

"I'll make her respect it again, you wait and see," Rey blustered. "When she and my precious brother find out what I've done for them, for all of us, they'll change their tune. They'll know who they owe, you watch. I won't be the screwup anymore, I'll be the one with vision."

"You've been chasing the wrong woman, you moron," Jack interrupted. "Sabrina Cromwell was taken from her hotel room days ago."

"Don't give me that," Rey protested. "I saw you and her standing at her hotel door. I saw her in the parking garage and outside her house."

"Who you saw is Sabrina's twin sister. You've been shooting at Sophia Sparrow, your older brother's former ticket to riches. Now she's missing, too. Guess who the cops want for both women's abductions?"

"Me?" Paul choked out, the bravado slipping from his voice.

"Yeah, and for a murder down in Seaport, too. You're a real popular guy right now." Jack walked him to his own car, where he opened the trunk and took out his bag of supplies. His gun was still in his shoulder holster but he dug out handcuffs and used them and a lot of threats to secure a swearing, kicking Rey's arms around a small but substantial tree.

"What time today did you leave the origami on Sabrina's porch?" he asked.

"Wait a second," Rey said, his face buried in bark. He tried to look back over his shoulder at Jack. "I have nothing to do with either girl's disappearance."

"Answer my question."

He sputtered moss and bark from his lips. "This morning. I left it this morning. Then I went to the hospital. Honest. When she left, I followed her to the house but she went in the back door and didn't even see the fox. That's my calling card, you know, because Reynard is pronounced like *renard*, which is—"

"French for *fox*. Yeah, I know."

"The dollar bill signifies her only value in the world."

Jack's jaw knotted. "What else did you see?"

"Nothing. I decided to wait and get her when she came back outside but then this dude showed up in a van. He disappeared around the side."

"Was there anything funny about the way he walked?"

"I wasn't watching him walk. I was watching the front door for the girl. Instead, all the lights go off in the house, then he comes back to the front and knocks out the window. In he goes. The next thing I know, out he comes with the girl over his shoulder. He threw her in the back of a van and off they went."

"You must have seen him then. Did he limp?"

"I don't know, I swear. It was dark and raining and I was—"

"Did you follow him?"

"Yeah. But I lost him. I decided to go back to the hospital but then your car drove right past me so I followed you back to the house. Take these handcuffs off," he begged. "My arms are killing me."

"Too bad." Jack thrust the muzzle of his gun against Rey's spine to emphasize his point. "Exactly where did you lose the van? I swear if you lie to me, come spring, the park rangers are going find your rotting corpse still hugging this tree."

"I'll tell you the truth, I swear," Paul Rey shouted. "Just stop poking me with that gun!"

"Start talking," Jack said.

SOPHIE AWOKE IN a twilight space surrounded by cinder block walls. She groaned when she moved her head. A tsunami of nausea rose in her throat and she rolled over on hands and knees to throw up.

Where was she?

She remembered a man coming through the broken glass, remembered big hands, a cloth—

She hadn't seen the guy's face. She wasn't sure if he was Adam Cook or Louis Nash or someone else entirely, just that it wasn't Paul Rey.

A nearby moan drew her attention. It seemed to come from what appeared to be a pile of cast-off clothes in the corner. She found she was not restrained and crawled the distance to discover the rags covered the body of another woman.

Sophie turned the woman's face toward the light coming through the two inches between the bottom of the door and the threshold. Even in the murky light, even with the woman's bloody split lip, her face streaked with dirt and caked with blood from an angry red slash down one cheek, Sophie recognized her. She'd seen that face every day for the past twenty-six years when she caught her own reflection in a mirror.

"Sabrina?" she whispered. *At last.*

Sabrina's trembling lips were her only response. Sophie discovered her sister was naked beneath the pile of clothes, her body bruised, her left leg swollen with what appeared to be a bullet wound in her thigh. The wound was infected. Alarmed, she touched Sabrina's forehead and found it dry and hot. "Oh, Sabrina," she said.

"Water," Sabrina moaned. Sophie's gaze traveled in every direction. The room itself was small, empty, dank, cold. Besides herself and Sabrina, the only object she could see was an overturned metal bucket with an attached length of chain as though it had been yanked from a well. She walked first to the door to pull on the knob. Surprise, the door didn't budge. She picked up the bucket, wincing at the clattering sound the chain made as it hit metal on metal, stilling it by grasping the links.

The bucket smelled horrible but she extended her fingers into the murky depths until she touched a substance near the bottom that felt almost as thick as mud. She took the bucket back to her sister's side and sat down.

"Water," Sabrina moaned again.

"Hang on," Sophie said as she pulled out the hem of her thermal shirt from beneath her sweater and scooped a handful of the muddy substance onto the box weave of the garment. She tightened the cloth around it and squeezed. Moisture dripped out. She held the gooey wad over Sabrina's face and directed a few precious drops onto her sister's dry lips. Undoubtedly it was filthy and germ laden but that seemed like the least of their problems at the moment. Sabrina's dry lips parted and she swallowed. Sophie repeated the process until at last Sabrina opened her eyes.

"Hello," Sophie whispered, taking her sister's hand.

"It's true," Sabrina gasped softly as she examined Sophie's face. Her voice was hoarse as though she'd screamed for days. Of course she'd screamed for days.

Five days to be exact. "He told me he saw *me*. Not here but somewhere else. I thought he was crazy. I—I didn't believe him."

"Who is he?" Sophie asked.

"I don't know," she said, her words slow in coming and because of the split lip, hard to understand. "Sometimes he says the word *darkroom*. I don't know if he means himself or this…this place."

She started trembling then and her grip on Sophie's hand tightened.

"We're going to get out of here," Sophie said.

"I tried to escape—a day or two ago, I tried. But he shot me and dragged me back here… Oh, I'm so sorry you're here, too. How is this possible?"

"Jack Travers and I have been looking for you."

"Jack?"

"Yes. We met because of you, and we fell in love because of you. Buzz is on his way home—"

"Buzz!" Sabrina cried as tears welled in her eyes. She raised a shaky hand to wipe them away. "My Buzz?"

My Buzz. The hope in those two words flooded Sophie's heart and in that instant she faced the fact that rescuing Sabrina and herself was the only way she would ever see Jack again. *Her Jack.*

"Buzz is coming," she repeated. "And you know what Jack is like. He'll never give up looking for us. But we have to do our part. Can you sit up?"

With Sophie's help, Sabrina struggled into a sitting position where at last Sophie could drape her with some of the discarded clothes to ward off the cold. "How did you escape before?" she asked.

"I jumped him." She licked her lips and frowned. "He comes with a rifle now and locks the door."

"What's on the other side of that door?"

"A small room…a horrible room…then another one filled with old appliances and junk. The exit leads into a forest." She touched Sophie's hair. "What's your name?"

"Sophia. I go by Sophie."

"We're identical twins?"

"Yes."

"My mother told me she heard a rumor after she adopted me that there were two babies but she was told the records had been destroyed. She tried but she could never find out anything else."

"The rumor was true."

Sabrina reached up and touched Sophie's hair. "I dye mine to get it as dark as yours."

"I dye mine, too," Sophie said.

Sabrina smiled. "You couldn't stand the mousy brown either?"

"I did for years but suddenly, I just couldn't."

Sabrina's free hand fell to her lap. "I always wanted a twin. I used to think what fun it would be to trick my parents into mistaking one of us for the other."

"We'll make up for lost time after we escape," Sophie said, her voice distracted, the wheels in her head suddenly turning.

"Escape? How?"

"It's going to require a lot out of you," Sophie said

slowly as she looked her sister in the eye. Was the poor woman up to it?

"Anything, anything to see Buzz again."

What other choice did they have? "Good." Sophie pulled her sweater over her head and then her thermal shirt. She took off her bra and shivered in the cold. "We're going to trade places," she said.

"No. No," Sabrina protested. "You don't know what he's like, what he'll do. I can't let you—"

"Shh," Sophie said. "He'll do all that anyway if we don't stop him. This is our chance and we're going to take it." She tore the clean hospital bandages off her arm and stuffed them out of sight. The cold room got even colder as she pulled off her boots and socks, then jeans…everything. If Sabrina had endured this man stark naked, so would she. It was what he expected to find and she would give it to him.

Dressing Sabrina was tricky. Between the injuries, the fear and the fever from her infection, she hurt everywhere. At last Sophie took off the pearl necklace her father had given her and fastened it around Sabrina's neck.

"This isn't going to fool him," Sabrina whispered. "He'll never let it happen. He's excited about having two of us. He has terrible plans."

"So do I," Sophie said with as much confidence as she could muster. She took off the silver earrings Danny had given her a lifetime ago.

"My ears aren't pierced," Sabrina muttered.

"That's okay. I need a cut on my face and I can't think of any other way to get it." She gripped one of the silver disks and scoured its edge back and forth against a protruding cinder block in the wall.

"You're making a blade," Sabrina said through chattering teeth.

"Yeah. But you're going to have to help me."

She ground the silver until the edge looked ragged enough to tear skin and then handed it to Sabrina, whose hand shook as she grasped it. Sophie touched her own face from the top of her right cheekbone down to her jaw near the bottom of her ear. "Put some muscle in it and remember you're saving my life, okay? That's what you firefighters do, right?"

Sabrina took the earring and held it to Sophie's cheek. Her hand fell. "I can't," she said after a moment.

"Yes, you can. I'll help you." She put her stronger hand over Sabrina's. Together, they managed to cut deep enough to spill warm blood down Sophie's cheek and throat. The pain was almost unbearable and it took every ounce of courage Sophie had not to tear the makeshift blade away from her skin. When it was done, she scooped up a handful of the mud in the bucket, then rubbed it over her face to approximate Sabrina's condition and in her hair to disguise the lilac streak. She wrapped a bloody piece of the clothing around her thigh as though she'd bandaged the gunshot wound. Next she added mud to cover the stitches in her arm. She was going to be on antibiotics for a month after this.

If there was an *after this…*

One of the hardest things she'd ever done was not put on every rag lying at her feet. Instead, she helped

Sabrina to stand and slowly walked her to the place she'd woken up minutes before. After helping her sit, she finger-combed Sabrina's hair. "Keep the cut side of your face against the knee you can bend so he doesn't see it," she cautioned. "With any luck he'll think you're still out. I'm still out, I mean."

She went back to the pile of rags and hid her newly made blade. If it tore her skin it would tear his. Then she picked up the bucket to go replace it but at that moment the not-so-distant sound of a banging door and heavy footsteps drove her heart into her throat. She glanced at Sabrina, who sagged against the wall toward the floor.

The footsteps grew closer as Sophie huddled under the heap of rags.

THE RAINY, MOONLESS night was as dark as the inside of an abandoned well. The only saving grace was the fact that Jack had been here once already today. He kept his headlights off and his foot soft on the accelerator, willing the car to creep up the long driveway without making a sound. While there was no moonlight to expose him as he got to the clearing, there was also no light to help him find his way. Better to be on foot than in a big machine if he crashed into anything. He shut off the interior lights and opened the door to merge into the rainy night like a shadow.

What killed him was the uncertainty that came with taking the word of a delusional sleaze like Paul Rey. He was here at this house on this night with nothing but the word of a convicted man, a man who had tried to kill

Sophie multiple times, a man without a conscience or a moral compass. For all he knew, Paul Rey had made up this story to cover his own tracks. He might have already shot Sophie.

He couldn't think like that. He'd heard on the radio that the guy with the stolen plates was leading half the police on a merry chase into Washington. Now the Washington police were involved, as well. Sabrina or Sophie could be in that car, not with Rey because that loser was still handcuffed to a tree, but maybe with Nash or Cook or even a faceless, nameless fourth man. Jack didn't want police to drop that ball to chase this one. It all came back as it did every time—how did you trust a guy like Paul Rey to tell you the truth?

You didn't. You checked it out yourself and called for backup when you had facts. That in this case backup meant "blazing gun" Leroy Donner, well, that was a sobering thought.

The house was as dark and foreboding as the night. He paused as he stood beside the car listening, trying to hear anything but the sound of the rain. Should he break in and search the place?

A light suddenly went on in the distance behind the cover of a few trees. He'd already taken the rifle out of his trunk and grabbed that now before silently closing the driver's door and starting toward the light.

The first thing he managed to do was trip over an invisible boulder that lined the drive—he'd forgotten they were there. He made his way toward the barn, his eyes on the light in case it was extinguished and he had to go from memory.

The building was open, unlocked, the interior light flooding a small patch of muddy ground outside. Jack took his time approaching the door, making sure no one was waiting for him. The hair on the back of his neck stood on end and he reminded himself it wasn't just Rey who sent him here, it was his own gut. He'd made a promise to himself after Lisa—he would listen to his instincts.

Once he was pretty sure he wasn't walking into an ambush, he entered what looked like a twelve-by-twelve room. Three upright freezers were lined up against two of the walls. A table used for butchering, if the floor drain and rusty-looking stains were any indication, sat against a third. A dangling unlit lamp hung over the table.

Gruesome.

And ominous, made more so by the gray-and-black duffel bag sitting atop the table. Louis Nash's bag, last seen in his office, retrieved from behind a locked door. Jack walked silently to the bag and found it unzipped. Inside he saw a picture that momentarily stunned him. Obviously taken through a window, a bloodied Sophie lay on the sidewalk, Jack hovering over her. And under her picture, he found the head shot of Sabrina and all the other women he'd last seen in Louis Nash's file cabinet along with the list of names under the heading Cases.

Paul Rey hadn't been lying. Louis Nash had taken Sophie and Sabrina, too.

He moved the papers and discovered the reason the duffel bag had clanked when Nash dropped it. The bag was filled with tools, including long serrated knives, saws, clamps and what appeared to be surgical implements. Some of it looked like things he remembered from the one and only time he'd helped a friend clean and dress a deer. They all sent chills down his spine.

The sound of a lock opening farther inside the structure caught his attention. He needed to hurry but there was no way he was leaving this room without checking out those freezers. He quickly opened the nearest and found it empty. He opened the one standing next to it and stared at its frozen contents for an interminable moment without breathing.

Shock and repulsion made him slam the door without consideration of noise. Holding the rifle in front of himself, he moved through the doorway toward the sound of the lock and into a dimly lit room dominated by a filthy mattress. Manacles were chained to the walls. Photographs of women in obvious agony loomed over the mattress like tortured souls caught in limbo. A camera sat on the mattress as if ready for use.

There was another door on the far side of the room.

From behind that door, he heard the low grumblings of a man's voice. He raised the rifle and moved to the door. He could see that it was locked. The only quick way through the lock was with a bullet but he didn't want that bullet to hit someone on the other side because there wasn't a doubt in his mind that Sophie was back there and maybe, maybe, Sabrina, too.

The matter was settled when a heart-wrenching scream cut through his heart.

SOPHIE SAW THE dark shape of two feet as they arrived on the other side of the door. She heard the jangle of the lock and then the creak of the wood as the door swung inward. Too late she wondered if she should have positioned herself right there by the door. No, no, he would have anticipated that. It was probably why it was taking him so long to enter.

What she had hoped was that this might be the one time he wouldn't lock the door behind him but that was not to be the case.

She heard his limp as he approached, but instead of coming to her, he walked over to Sabrina. She could see him through one eye if she squinted. He stopped before her sister's sitting form, grabbed her hair and pulled her face up to look at it. Surely he would see the cut on Sabrina's cheek. Her heart sank down to the depths of hell.

"Wake up," he said and kicked what Sophie realized was Sabrina's injured leg. Sabrina didn't respond. She had to have passed out. He moved toward Sophie. She steeled herself.

"Okay, bitch," he whispered as he stood over her. "I'll start with you."

He leaned down to grab her. She made herself go limp as he pulled her to her feet, a rifle in one hand, his other hand clamped around her arm. She held the makeshift blade so firmly she was pretty sure it was cutting through her own skin. She made a few appropriately weak-sounding noises and sagged as though too hurt to move on her own. He ran his hands over her body like he owned her. Then he leaned down and hoisted her over his shoulder and took a struggled step toward the door.

And that's when she dug the blade into the side of his neck, aiming for his jugular vein or his carotid artery—she didn't care just as long as it stopped him.

He flung her away from himself. She hit the floor with a bone-cracking thud. A moment later he was on top of her, blood dripping unheeded down his neck and into his clothes. She fought him but he was unimaginably strong. He pinned her to the floor and sat atop her, the rifle still gripped in his hand, a smile now toying with his lips.

From over his shoulder she saw Sabrina's face. She'd somehow managed to stand on her own and grab the bucket. She held a length of its attached chain between her hands. Nash seemed hell-bent on dominating Sophie and to keep it that way she spit up into his face. The spit didn't quite make it but the gesture infuriated him. As he raised a hand to pummel her, Sabrina threw the chain around his neck. In her weakened condition, she was no match for this monster. He rose in one fluid motion to his feet, shaking Sabrina off his back like a piece of lint. She hit the wall with a piercing scream.

Sophie took the second he was distracted by Sabrina to grab the abandoned bucket. She flung the chain over his head again and managed to get it around his neck but he was too tall and the chain too thick for her to tighten it into a stranglehold. He roared as he freed himself, his face crimson as he shook her away. She searched the floor for her makeshift blade but couldn't see it. A string of oaths filled the room as he grabbed Sophie's leg and dragged her toward the door. Her muddy foot slipped from his grasp and she crawled back to Sabrina's side. He was going to kill both of them in this hellhole if she didn't do something to stop it but she was out of tricks and opportunities...

A shot thundered in the small room and for a second, Sophie thought Louis Nash had fired it. But neither she nor Sabrina had been hit and Nash had frozen in place. As he turned toward the door, she once again grabbed the bucket and found the chain. Another shot boomed. As Nash fell backward, she threw the bucket aside and scuttled to pull Sabrina out of his way.

Footsteps broke the almost deafening silence and Sophie looked up to find Jack framed in the doorway. A sob of relief choked her as he crossed quickly to Louis Nash's downed body, kicked the rifle away and knelt.

The big man lay as still as stone. Jack stood.

"Sophie," he whispered as he crossed to her. He fell to his knees, his gun still trained on Nash. With a glance at Sabrina, he whispered, "How is she?"

"Alive," Sophie said through the tears rolling down her cheeks. "Alive."

"Thank goodness."

He gently touched Sophie's bloodied cheek before shrugging off his wet but blessedly warm jacket and draping it over her bare shoulders. His arm enfolded her as he pressed her against his chest and for a second, his grip was so tight she couldn't breathe.

Well, who needed to breathe when they'd been yanked from the yawning pit of the devil's throat to find themselves magically delivered to heaven? And wrapped in Jack's arms, that's exactly where she was.

"Let's get you both out of here," he whispered into her hair.

IT WAS ALMOST dawn and Jack sat in the hospital waiting room talking to Detective Reece. Sheriff Donner had come and gone like a boisterous windstorm, Sabrina was in recovery after surgery, Sophie was being treated and Buzz was stuck on the wrong side of a mudslide in his journey to the coast from the airport.

"Nash is going to make it," Reece said.

Jack, not trusting his voice or choice of words, just nodded.

"He got chatty. I think Sabrina is alive because of her car. Nash apparently stashed her in his van after he got her to open that hotel room door, drugged her and stuffed her in a trunk. Then he drove her car to a spot where he hid it. Next he drove his van up here with a slight detour to dump the handyman's body. He hitch-hiked back to Seaport. He retrieved her car and drove the back roads to Astoria and that took a while. By then two days had gone by. She tried to escape and he shot her. When he saw Sophie lying on the sidewalk, his warped mind built a lovely little scenario—well, you know what was in those freezers."

"Heads," Jack said woodenly, wishing the image

would magically disappear and knowing it never would. "Women's severed heads."

Reece nodded. "He's been nabbing women for years and bringing them back to that horrible, horrible place."

"What about his mother?"

"She's in the freezer, too. Nash has been cashing her social security checks."

"And Adam Cook's big secret," Jack said, "according to Sheriff Donner, who got a wild hair and went up to Cook's land tonight, is the meth lab he built on the back of his property. I should have guessed what he was up to when I saw that box of lantern fuel in his van."

Reece shook his head, met Jack's gaze and sighed deeply. "And I should have listened to you, Jack. I could have gotten both Sabrina and Sophie killed. If you want a job, by the way, it's yours."

Jack half smiled. "Thanks. Who knows, I may take you up on it. I don't think Sophie is going to want Sabrina out of her sight for a long time. They have some major catching up to do. But there's one more thing and that's Lisa. Nash said he lived in California years ago. He mentioned an ex-wife—"

"After you told me about that, I checked it out," Reece said. "The ex-wife lives in San Diego now and Nash was telling the truth, she did hound him for money that was rightfully hers. I don't know if we'll ever be able to trace Nash back to Lisa, but we'll do our best."

Jack nodded. As far as the law was concerned, their best would have to do. As for him—he *knew*. Not with proof but with his gut.

May Lisa finally rest in peace.

A figure appeared in the doorway, as tall as Jack, a little heavier, bearded and sunburned and wearing a parka that looked like it had become a second skin. Buzz Cromwell's gaze went directly to Jack, his gray eyes filled with worry. "Where is she?"

Jack got to his feet. "She's in recovery," he said as he went to hug his friend. "She was banged up pretty good, Buzz."

"I need to see her."

"Come sit down. Let me tell you what her doctor said."

The man came reluctantly, nodding a greeting at Reece, who muttered his farewells and left.

Buzz sat down heavily. "What did that creep do to her?"

"I don't know the details, but I do know she's had a harrowing time. The biggest physical problem was the shot to her leg, but that's going to mend. If anyone can get through this, she can, you know that."

A nurse motioned to them from the door. "Gentlemen," she said. "You can follow me."

As they got to Sabrina's room, Buzz paused, and Jack saw his gaze travel from Sophie, who stood holding Sabrina's hand, to Sabrina, whose swollen cracked lips curved when she saw him. Even through their individual scars and bandages there was no mistaking their likeness. Buzz rushed to Sabrina's side and leaned over her.

"I didn't want to worry you," she whispered.

He kissed her forehead. "I'm here now, sweetie. No

one's going to hurt you again, I promise." He laid his cheek against her forehead and closed his eyes.

Jack's gaze moved to Sophie, whom he found staring at him. She settled her sister's hand by her side and moved from around the bed. The nurses had helped her shower and lent her blue sweats. Her forehead and right cheek were bandaged and her skin was as white as ivory. By now he'd heard her story, what she'd done, and he wasn't sure if the glow that seemed to pour from her eyes came from the outside or the inside. Both, he decided.

He met her halfway and put his arms around her.

"Thank you for saving us," she whispered after a few moments.

"I love you, Sophie Sparrow," he said as he searched for a place to kiss her that wasn't bandaged. "I can't imagine a life without you."

"You don't have to," she said, and touched her lips to his. "I'm not going anywhere."

BEFORE A WEDDING could be accomplished, they decided Jack needed to return to California to tie up loose ends and Sabrina had to get well enough to act as Sophie's maid of honor. On the day Sabrina was finally being released from the hospital, the two sisters found themselves sitting side by side on the bed. Sophie had been on the phone and now she clicked it off and turned to her twin. "Grandpa is expecting us next weekend," she said. "Jack will be home by then so maybe all four of us could drive up there together to see him."

Sabrina nodded. "I could use a short road trip. What does our grandfather want?"

"He's anxious to discuss our inheritance and the house and the island—all of that."

Sabrina's smile was wistful. "That's nice. What I really want to know from him is what our birth mother was like, if he knows who our father is, if we have any other family—that kind of stuff."

"Me, too," Sophie said. Then she added, "Whether or not we do we both have something we didn't have before."

"Each other," they said in unison.

* * * * *

Don't miss the previous book from Alice Sharpe:

Hidden Identity

Available now from Harlequin Intrigue!

HICNM0619

Get 4 FREE REWARDS!

We'll send you 2 FREE Books plus 2 FREE Mystery Gifts.

Harlequin Intrigue® books feature heroes and heroines that confront and survive danger while finding themselves irresistibly drawn to one another.

FREE
Value Over
$20

YES! Please send me 2 FREE Harlequin Intrigue® novels and my 2 FREE gifts (gifts are worth about $10 retail). After receiving them, if I don't wish to receive any more books, I can return the shipping statement marked "cancel." If I don't cancel, I will receive 6 brand-new novels every month and be billed just $4.99 each for the regular-print edition or $5.74 each for the larger-print edition in the U.S., or $5.74 each for the regular-print edition or $6.49 each for the larger-print edition in Canada. That's a savings of at least 12% off the cover price! It's quite a bargain! Shipping and handling is just 50¢ per book in the U.S. and 75¢ per book in Canada.* I understand that accepting the 2 free books and gifts places me under no obligation to buy anything. I can always return a shipment and cancel at any time. The free books and gifts are mine to keep no matter what I decide.

Choose one: ☐ **Harlequin Intrigue®**
Regular-Print
(182/382 HDN GMYW)

☐ **Harlequin Intrigue®**
Larger-Print
(199/399 HDN GMYW)

Name (please print)

Address   Apt. #

City   State/Province   Zip/Postal Code

Mail to the **Reader Service:**
IN U.S.A.: P.O. Box 1341, Buffalo, NY 14240-8531
IN CANADA: P.O. Box 603, Fort Erie, Ontario L2A 5X3

Want to try 2 free books from another series! Call 1-800-873-8635 or visit www.ReaderService.com.

---

*Terms and prices subject to change without notice. Prices do not include sales taxes, which will be charged (if applicable) based on your state or country of residence. Canadian residents will be charged applicable taxes. Offer not valid in Quebec. This offer is limited to one order per household. Books received may not be as shown. Not valid for current subscribers to Harlequin Intrigue books. All orders subject to approval. Credit or debit balances in a customer's account(s) may be offset by any other outstanding balance owed by or to the customer. Please allow 4 to 6 weeks for delivery. Offer available while quantities last.

Your Privacy—The Reader Service is committed to protecting your privacy. Our Privacy Policy is available online at www.ReaderService.com or upon request from the Reader Service. We make a portion of our mailing list available to reputable third parties that offer products we believe may interest you. If you prefer that we not exchange your name with third parties, or if you wish to clarify or modify your communication preferences, please visit us at www.ReaderService.com/consumerschoice or write to us at Reader Service Preference Service, P.O. Box 9062, Buffalo, NY 14240-9062. Include your complete name and address.

HI19R2

INTRIGUE

One night, when Mary Cardwell Savage is lonely, she sends a letter to Chase Steele, her first love. Little does she know that this action will bring both Chase and his psychotic ex-girlfriend into her life...

Read on for a sneak preview of
Steel Resolve *by* New York Times *and* USA TODAY *bestselling author B.J. Daniels.*

The moment Fiona found the letter in the bottom of Chase's sock drawer, she knew it was bad news. Fear squeezed the breath from her as her heart beat so hard against her rib cage that she thought she would pass out. Grabbing the bureau for support, she told herself it might not be what she thought it was.

But the envelope was a pale lavender, and the handwriting was distinctly female. Worse, Chase had kept the letter a secret. Why else would it be hidden under his socks? He hadn't wanted her to see it because it was from that other woman.

Now she wished she hadn't been snooping around. She'd let herself into his house with the extra key she'd had made. She'd felt him pulling away from her the past few weeks. Having been here so many times before, she was determined that this one wasn't going to break her heart. Nor was she going to let another woman take him from her. That's why she had to find out why he hadn't called, why he wasn't returning her messages, why he was avoiding her.

They'd had fun the night they were together. She'd felt as if they had something special, although she knew the next morning that he was feeling guilty. He'd said he didn't want to lead her on. He'd told her that there was some woman back home he was still in love with. He'd said their night together was a mistake. But he was wrong, and she was determined to convince him of it.

What made it so hard was that Chase was a genuinely nice guy. You didn't let a man like that get away. The other woman had. Fiona wasn't going to make that mistake, even though he'd been trying to push her away since that night. But he had no idea how determined she could be, determined enough for both of them that this wasn't over by a long shot.

It wasn't the first time she'd let herself into his apartment when he was at work. The other time, he'd caught her and she'd had to make up some story about the building manager letting her in so she could look for her lost earring.

She'd snooped around his house the first night they'd met—the same night she'd found his extra apartment key and had taken it to have her own key made in case she ever needed to come back when Chase wasn't home.

The letter hadn't been in his sock drawer that time.

That meant he'd received it since then. Hadn't she known he was hiding something from her? Why else would he put this letter in a drawer instead of leaving it out along with the bills he'd casually dropped on the table by the front door?

Because the letter was important to him, which meant that she had no choice but to read it.

Don't miss
Steel Resolve *by B.J. Daniels,*
available July 2019 wherever
Harlequin® Intrigue books and ebooks are sold.

www.Harlequin.com

HIEXP0619

Need an adrenaline rush from nail-biting tales
(and irresistible males)?

Check out **Harlequin Intrigue®**,
Harlequin® Romantic Suspense and
Love Inspired® Suspense books!

New books available every month!

CONNECT WITH US AT:

Facebook.com/groups/HarlequinConnection

 Facebook.com/HarlequinBooks

Twitter.com/HarlequinBooks

 Instagram.com/HarlequinBooks

Pinterest.com/HarlequinBooks

ReaderService.com

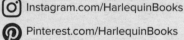

**ROMANCE WHEN
YOU NEED IT**

SGENRE2018R

SPECIAL EXCERPT FROM

HQN™

*Garrett Sterling has a second chance at love
with the woman he could never forget.
Can he keep both of them alive long enough
to see if their relationship has a future?*

Read on for a sneak preview of
Luck of the Draw, *the second book in the
Sterling's Montana series by* New York Times
and USA TODAY *bestselling author B.J. Daniels.*

Garrett Sterling brought his horse up short as something across
the deep ravine caught his eye. A fierce wind swayed the towering
pines against the mountainside as he dug out his binoculars. He
could smell the rain in the air. Dark clouds had gathered over the
top of Whitefish Mountain. If he didn't turn back soon, he would
get caught in the summer thunderstorm. Not that he minded it
all that much, except the construction crew working at the guest
ranch would be anxious for the weekend and their paychecks.
Most in these parts didn't buy into auto deposit.

Even as the wind threatened to send his Stetson flying and he
felt the first few drops of rain dampen his long-sleeved Western
shirt, he couldn't help being curious about what he'd glimpsed.
He'd seen something moving through the trees on the other side
of the ravine.

He raised the binoculars to his eyes, waiting for them to
focus. "What the hell?" When he'd caught movement, he'd been
expecting elk or maybe a deer. If he was lucky, a bear. He hadn't
seen a grizzly in this area in a long time, but it was always a good
idea to know if one was around.

But what had caught his eye was human. He was too startled to
breathe for a moment. A large man moved through the pines. He

wasn't alone. He had hold of a woman's wrist in what appeared to be a death grip and was dragging her behind him. She seemed to be struggling to stay on her feet. It was what he saw in the man's other hand that had stolen his breath. A gun.

Garrett couldn't believe what he was seeing. Surely, he was wrong. Through the binoculars, he tried to keep track of the two. But he kept losing them as they moved through the thick pines. His pulse pounded as he considered what to do.

His options were limited. He was too far away to intervene and he had a steep ravine between him and the man with the gun. Nor could he call for help—as if help could arrive in time. There was no cell phone coverage this far back in the mountains outside of Whitefish, Montana.

Through the binoculars, he saw the woman burst out of the trees and realized that she'd managed to break away from the man. For a moment, Garrett thought she was going to get away. But the man was larger and faster and was on her quickly, catching her and jerking her around to face him. He hit her with the gun, then put the barrel to her head as he jerked her to him.

"No!" Garrett cried, the sound lost in the wind and crackle of thunder in the distance. After dropping the binoculars onto his saddle, he drew his sidearm from the holster at his hip and fired a shot into the air. It echoed across the wide ravine, startling his horse.

As he struggled to holster the pistol again and grab the binoculars, a shot from across the ravine filled the air, echoing back at him.

Don't miss
Luck of the Draw *by B.J. Daniels, available June 2019 wherever Harlequin® books and ebooks are sold.*

www.Harlequin.com

Love Harlequin romance?

DISCOVER.

Be the first to find out about promotions,
news and exclusive content!

Facebook.com/HarlequinBooks

Twitter.com/HarlequinBooks

Instagram.com/HarlequinBooks

Pinterest.com/HarlequinBooks

ReaderService.com

EXPLORE.

Sign up for the Harlequin e-newsletter and
download a free book from any series at
TryHarlequin.com.

CONNECT.

Join our Harlequin community to share
your thoughts and connect with other
romance readers!
Facebook.com/groups/HarlequinConnection

HARLEQUIN®

**ROMANCE WHEN
YOU NEED IT**

HSOCIAL2018